Acclaim for

The Prophet of Zongo Street

"With clear, direct prose . . . Ali delivers an amalgam of modern life and ancient tradition. Unique scenes and descriptions . . . give a palpable richness to stories circling rhythmically around difficult and intriguing issues." —*Richmond Times-Dispatch*

"Ali skillfully crafts characters whose warmth and familiarity entice the reader. . . . Ali writes like a butterfly." —*Entertainment Weekly*

"A collection of rich and resonant stories, haunting and ultimately hopeful in their commitment to the truth." —*O* magazine

"Lively, polished stories. . . . Ali shows almost anthropological interest in his characters, and a keen eye for the humanistic detail." —*Kirkus Reviews* (starred)

"Imaginistic, muscular, superb."

—Barry Hannah, author of *Airships* and *Ray*

"With his acute intelligence and cultural awareness, Ali is certain to become one of the representative West African sensibilities of his generation . . . as in an earlier generation a writer such as Chinua Achebe was able to offer."

—James Lasdun, author of *The Horned Man*

"Direct and rhythmically dextrous, Ali's writing has a kind of folkloric quality I associate with African writers I know well—Amos Tutuola, for example. [But] I really love its politics and philosophical intentions." —Rick Moody, author of *Garden State*

THE PROPHET OF ZONGO STREET

Stories

MOHAMMED NASEEHU ALI

AMISTAD
An Imprint of HarperCollins*Publishers*

A portion of "Mallam Sile" first appeared in *The New Yorker*.

A hardcover edition of this book was published in 2005 by Amistad, an imprint of HarperCollins Publishers.

First Amistad paperback edition published 2006.

Designed by Claire Naylon Vaccaro

The Library of Congress has cataloged the hardcover edition as follows:

Ali, Mohammed Naseehu.
The prophet of Zongo Street : stories / Mohammed Naseehu Ali.—1st ed.
p. cm.
Contents: The story of day and night—The prophet of Zongo Street—Live-in—The Manhood test—The true Aryan—Ward G-4—Rachmaninov—Mallam Sile—Faith—Man pass man.
ISBN 0-06-052354-9 (Alk. paper)
1. Ghana—Social life and customs—Fiction.   I. Title.

PR9379.9.A37P76   2005
823'.92—dc22   2004062722

ISBN-13: 978-0-06-088750-6 (pbk.)
ISBN-10: 0-06-088750-8

06 07 08 09 10 BVG/RRD 10 9 8 7 6 5 4 3 2 1

To my mother, Fatima Bintu Imam,
and my father, Sarki Abubakar Ali III, Emir of Zongo—
in loving memories

ACKNOWLEDGMENTS

My sincere thanks to the following people for their advice and support: Dawn Davis, Rone Shavers, Stacey Barney, Jim Rutman, Fawzeeyah Ali, Laila Abubakar Ali, Rick Moody, Charles Bock, Nick Bozanic, Terry Caszatt, Michael Delp, Reginald McKnight, Ted Hoagland, James Lasdun, Joshua Cohen, Janice Crockett, and Omar Farouk Ibraheem. Also, I am grateful to Ledig House International Writers' Residency for providing me with a room and a cook when I most needed them in order to complete work on this book.

Every soul will taste of death. And ye will be paid on the Day of Resurrection only that which ye have fairly earned. Whoso is removed from the fire and is made to enter Paradise, he indeed is triumphant. The life of this world is but comfort of illusion.

THE GLORIOUS QUR'AN 3:185
TRANSLATION BY MOHAMMAD M. PICKTHALL

Contents

CONTENTS

THE STORY OF
DAY AND NIGHT

For four nights Uwargida did not appear at her regular spot in the courtyard, where she narrated Mallam Gizo, or Mr. Spider tales and other mythological stories to us every night. Uwargida was one of the four widowed grandmothers who lived in our house on Zongo Street, a densely populated section of Kumasi, Ghana's most prosperous city. Each of the four old women were at one time married to Father's father, the Hausa king, who died some thirty years ago, when Father himself was only eleven years old. Uwargida's name means "mother of the house," which was exactly what she was: the king's first wife and the oldest of the four wives. She was ninety-one.

The last night we saw Uwargida, she had promised to tell us "the story that began it all," the story of how light and darkness came about on earth. "It's the most chilling story ever," she had exclaimed in her raspy and rather thin voice as we escorted her back to her quarters that night. Grandmother Kande told me that Uwargida's knees were bothering her once again,

and that was why she had not made it down to the courtyard in
the past few nights.

"Now, don't you kids go disturbing Yaya Uwargida up there;
her body has been arguing with her lately," shouted Grand-
mother Kande from her verandah, when she saw a host of chil-
dren, myself included, sneaking our way up toward Uwargida's
quarters.

"No, no, we are just going to pray for her knees to feel better,"
said Sumaila, our spokesperson. Grandmother Kande nodded,
giving us the go-ahead. We all giggled, happy that we had out-
smarted Grandmother Kande again, and quickly made our way
up the small concrete hill that led to Uwargida's side of the big
compound.

Once we were in her room, we tried to convince Uwargida
that it was indeed good for her health to come out and tell us the
story she had promised. "The gentle breeze will make you feel
better," coaxed the sweet-mouthed Sumaila.

"It's the truth Sumaila is speaking, Uwargida," chirped in all
of us, to put more pressure on the old woman. Moments later—
after a feeble attempt to drive us out of her room with her
cane—Uwargida decided to come with us. "All right, all right,
but one of you should go and tell Barkisu to prepare charcoal
fire," she said while struggling to lift herself off the nylon mat.
(Barkisu was Uwargida's servant girl.) We grinned wildly at each
other, excited that not only was Uwargida going to come out and
tell us the story, but she was also going to make us her freshly
roasted groundnut, the best in all of the city of Kumasi, and fa-
mous because of a secret ingredient and a special red sand she
used, which gave the nuts a perfect crunch and an earthy smell.

By the time Uwargida made her way slowly down to the center of the house, more than thirty of us kids were already gathered around the charcoal fire. Some twenty minutes later, after the first batch of groundnuts had been distributed to everyone, the "mother of the house" was ready to tell us "the mother of all stories." The story of day and night.

"*Gáta na, gáta nanku,*" Uwargida began with the traditional opening line, inviting us to give her our full attention.

"*Tajé, takómó,*" we responded in a loud chorus, our mouths full of groundnuts.

"*Manymany* years ago," she continued in a soft, yet commanding voice. "During the time of our ancestors' ancestors' ancestors, when the universe was first created, there lived a childless woman whose name was Baadiya.

"At that time, all the different creations, humans, jinns, and the angels lived together in the same space, and they interacted with each other. The angels and jinns roamed about the skies freely, without any need for food, water, or air; and they lived forever. It was the same story with humans. We, too, lived forever back then, though unlike the angels and jinns, we needed food and water to survive. And also, there was neither day nor night and neither daylight nor darkness, as we have now. The universe was made up of a grayish, reddish fog, a sight that was hard to describe" Uwargida paused, as if to allow what she had said so far to sink into our heads.

"And it was in a small village in one of the lands of this universe that Baadiya lived with her husband," she continued, amid the cracking noises made by the groundnut husks being popped open. "Every woman in this village, with the exception of Baadiya, had a child. It was all the more sad, because Baadiya was a very kind woman and also her husband's first wife. But when she didn't have a child within two years of their union, the husband married a second wife, a third wife, and even added a fourth one. The husband wanted more children, and so each new wife got pregnant as soon as she stepped into his house. Before long, the three wives were jeering at Baadiya for not having a child of her own. And anytime they had a little quarrel or fight, the wives were apt to remind Baadiya of her childlessness. After a while Baadiya couldn't stand the pain and suffering any longer, and she decided to seek the help of medicine men.

"She visited all the shrines and oracles of the fetish priests in the land, seeking help, but none of them was able to assist her. They told her they had no child to give at that time. Eventually Baadiya took her cries to Kato, who was half jinn and half angel and also the most powerful fetish priest in the land.

"After listening to Baadiya's story in silence, Kato broke the sad news to Baadiya that her problem was a human problem, and that unless she wanted a *dan-aljanni* like him, she should take her case to a human spiritualist.

" 'But I have been to all of them, and no one was able to help me,' " cried Baadiya.

" 'I know, woman,' " empathized Kato. " 'But you human animals are different from us jinns and angels. You see, we don't have blood in our veins like you do, and when we want to have a child, we just utter the two words *Child be!* and a ready-made young *jinn* or angel appears in front of us. We don't have to wait three months, as you humans do,' Kato said."

"Three months? Isn't it nine?" asked Asana, the orphan girl, who sat next to me on the mat.

"No, back then it took women three months to carry babies in their wombs," answered Uwargida.

As a nine-year-old, I was still grappling with the idea of how human beings were conceived, and so thought of asking Uwargida to explain why and how the duration was increased to nine months. But remembering her ubiquitous cane, I decided to keep my mouth shut. Just then, one of the boys attempted to ask the old woman the same question I had had in mind, but Uwargida's cane was on his head before he even finished the sentence. The boy screamed in pain, "*Wayyo, Allah*," which drew laughter from us all.

"Where was I?" asked Uwargida, who seemed a bit distracted. No one said a word, but the old woman continued anyway.

"Ahaa, so after much persistence from Baadiya, Kato was moved by the profound sadness on her face, and he recommended a fetish priest who would be able to find her a child. " 'His name is Kantamanto, and his oracle, the oracle of the slippery sand, is your only hope, woman, as he calls to a higher deity and power,' Kato said to her. 'But the only problem is that his shrine is located *veryveryvery*, very far away—at the end of the universe, in the land where the sea and the sky all meet.'

" 'Baba, the distance and the danger are not a problem to me,' said Baadiya. Kato gave Baadiya the directions to the fetish. A few days later, she set out on her journey to the land where the sea and the sky all met.

"After traveling for a whole moon and a half, Baadiya reached the hut of Kantamanto, who had already been informed of

Baadiya's approach by spiritual bodies. After listening to Baadiya's story, the priest didn't waste any time in breaking the sad news she had heard all along, that he, too, had no child to give her. 'I am sorry, woman, all my children are out on long errands into the world,' " he told her.

"Of course Baadiya had not come all this way to take no for an answer. She fell to the ground and grabbed the feet of the fetish priest and sobbed: 'Can't you see how long I have suffered? What have I done to deserve this? Look at what has become of me, how wretched and useless I am. Even the most powerful jinn back in my land told me you are the only one capable of giving me a baby, and now you, too, are denying me. Please, help me.' "

"Kantamanto didn't say a word for a *longlong* time, during which he mumbled some mysterious phrases to himself. He then closed his eyes, and soon afterward, his lips started moving rapidly, like someone having a conversation with an invisible body. Baadiya stopped crying upon seeing that. She bowed her head in silence and waited for the priest to finish his chants. Moments later he opened his eyes, and he then began to speak.

" 'Young woman, it's not that I don't want to give you a child. I see your agony and understand your suffering. And, in fact, I even knew about it before you got here. But the only child I have at the moment is not a good child. He is a dangerous child; and with you being a good woman, to whom the Fates have already been most unkind, I don't want to add to your suffering by giving you a problem child.'

" 'You just give him to me, Baba. I don't care who he is or what he looks like. A bad child is better than none, after all.'

"The fetish tried to explain the dangerous nature of the

child, but Baadiya was deaf, so great was her desire and desperation. He even swore that if she returned in six months, he would have a better child for her. Some of my children on errand in the universe would have returned by then,' he told her. But true to the Hausa adage that says, 'One who is destined to receive a beating never listens to a word of caution,' Baadiya remained persistent. She begged and pleaded, and cried in hysterical fashion. In the end Kantamanto decided to give her the child, though before she left, he said this to her: 'You may live to regret this decision one day.'

" 'I am sorry, Baba, but my life has already been one of regret, nothing could make it worse,' she replied. The priest decided to grant Baadiya her wish. After a long, incomprehensible incantation, he produced a red-leathered talisman and handed it to her. 'Place this under your kapok as soon as you arrive home. Your child, a baby boy, will arrive nine months after you have entered your husband's room,' he told her.

"Baadiya was in such a hurry to leave the shrine and return home that she forgot to ask Kantamanto why her child was arriving in nine months, instead of three."

Uwargida coughed and made an agonizing face. She massaged her right knee, to relieve the ache and pain. Then she asked for some water, which was brought to her in a gourd. She grabbed some groundnuts from the bowl in front of her, popped them open, and tossed them in her mouth. Even though Uwargida had fewer than a dozen teeth left, she always managed to eat her nuts without any problem.

. . .

"Exactly nine months later, Baadiya gave birth to a baby boy," Uwargida resumed. "The little devil came out feet first, something the people immediately considered a bad sign. They had never seen such a thing before. And even though the baby was very small, it still took three old women to deliver him.

"On the third day following his birth, the child was named 'Mewuya' because of his unusually long neck. Mewuya grew rapidly, and was soon much bigger than all the other children his age. He was extremely quiet and very private, though he was not shy, per se. A loner, Mewuya often wandered into the bush all by himself, searching for tools to make his favorite 'plaything,' knives.

"At age seven Mewuya spent all day creating blades of various sizes and patterns, which he polished until they were shiny enough for him to see his face on their surfaces. When he was busy at work on his knives, Mewuya had an intense gaze that scared even grown-ups.

"A woman who had stared at him too long had begun to hallucinate. She told people she saw hundreds of little children just like Mewuya in her sleep, and that they all held knives and chased her around, even when she was awake. People told the poor, sad woman that she was just seeing things and that it had nothing to do with Mewuya. When the woman died suddenly, the people came to believe that the boy had a hand in it, and that he possessed evil powers; but no one dared confront him, as they all feared he might do to them what he did to this woman.

"Then one day, not long after Mewuya had reached nine years, he said to his mother, 'I desire to behead some chickens. Go and fetch me some.' Baadiya opened her mouth in shock from what she had heard. Not wanting others to hear their exchange, the mother took him inside the hut and sat him down.

" 'You want me to get you a chicken to behead just like that?' she asked.

" 'Yes,' the child answered rather nonchalantly. The fetish priest's warning came rushing into Baadiya's mind, and her heart sank into her stomach immediately, causing her abdominal pains and sweats.

" 'Are you hungry for chicken meat?' she asked, trying to disguise her fear.

" 'No,' he answered, and knowing that his mother would not give in to his wishes with a clear mind, Mewuya decided to use his secret powers to hypnotize her into doing what he desired. After staring into Baadiya's eyes for a brief moment, all the while invoking his yet unknown diety, Mewuya rendered his mother senseless, so he could control her.

"Soon after, it was Baadiya herself who said to her son, 'You want a chicken, wait here and I'll bring one to you.' She ran to the back of their hut and returned with a fowl to give to her son. A moment later the fowl's headless body was convulsing on the ground. Mewuya looked at his mother and demanded another chicken. Baadiya fetched it for him immediately.

"Within a short while, Mewuya had beheaded all the livestock owned by his mother and father. He went to the next house and asked for their animals, and in no time, he had finished with all of them. The compound was littered with the blood of headless goats, sheep, chicken, and ducks. He even killed the rabbits. Of course the guinea fowls flew away. Some ducks tried to flee, too, but their wings and fat bodies couldn't carry them very far. They landed back onto the ground, only to be picked up and slaughtered by the obsessed child. By the end of that day, Mewuya had beheaded all the animals in his neighborhood."

The late-evening chill was beginning to set in, and the fire was begining to die out. We covered ourselves with sleepcloths to keep warm. Some of us were getting scared by the macabre turn of Uwargida's tale, and in order to assuage our fears, each of us moved closer to the child who sat next to us. Though her rheumatism worsened with the night's cooler air, Uwargida seemed determined to finish the tale.

"The next day was no different from the previous one for the bloodthirsty young boy," Uwargida continued. "After finishing off the neighborhood's livestock, Mewuya moved his bloody binge on to other areas of the village, and in a few days, no living animal was found anywhere. Though utterly horrified by this bloody massacre, the people were somewhat relieved when the neck of the last animal fell. With no more animals to slaughter, they thought, Mewuya will have no choice but to put an end to his rampage. However, little did they know that the little boy would soon be demanding their own heads. And whose head do you think was the first he went for?" Uwargida asked softly. No response was heard from any of us, not even a cough.

"His mother's. His mother became his first human victim," Uwargida continued, answering her own question. "And he showed no sign of mercy in those devilish eyes when he slaughtered her."

"But, Yaya, why didn't she ask him to stop, or even run away?" I finally mustered the guts to ask a question.

"To run away? What makes you think anyone could run away from that devil? One look from him turned even the strongest and fiercest men into mere babies; he could do whatever he wished to them. And this devil child had only one wish in his life: to behead every single human being in the entire universe."

A chill ran up my spine, causing spasms in my upper body. Sumaila folded his arms in between his legs, and though he was obviously frightened, he tried to hide it with a fake grin, as if he was actually humored by the story's bloody details. Some of the kids were so scared, they sealed off their ears with their fingertips. The servant girl who sat next to me closed her eyes, as if the killer boy was right there in front of us. Often, some kids would fall asleep as soon as they had been given their share of Uwargida's groundnut. But not this night. Everyone, it seemed, was afraid even to blink an eye.

"After finishing off his mother, Mewuya didn't waste any time in beheading his father, whom he killed with a single strike of his sharpest and longest blade. After killing his parents, you all know the rest. Before the week could turn around, the child had beheaded every single person in the village and was ready to move on to other villages and towns in the land. Within a month he had killed every animal and every human being in every village in the universe, with the exception of the village in the land where the sea and the sky all met."

Uwargida coughed up some phlegm and spat it into the ash-filled spit-bowl in front of her. Using a stick, she stirred the pile, causing the sticky, yellowy mucus to blend with the ash.

"But Mewuya did not get his way with the people of this village, because Kantamanto—the same fetish priest who gave

Baadiya the birth medicine—had received last-minute help from Kato, the half-jinn half-angel fetish who steered Mewuya's mother to him in the first place.

"Though Kato knew of Mewuya's carnage as soon as it had started, he had no way of saving humanity immediately; the leader of all the jinns and angels in the universe was at that time engaged in very, very important cosmic work down under the deep sea. By the time he managed to send the medicine needed to challenge Mewuya's deviltry to Kantamanto, the boy had wiped out almost all the humans in the universe.

"Armed with Kato's medicine, and with the help of his own oracle—the Oracle of the Slippery Sand—Kantamanto was well prepared for Mewuya. The priest created special talismans, potions, and charms with which to challenge Mewuya's equally powerful medicine. So when Mewuya showed up in the land at the end of the world and ordered everyone to step out to be beheaded, the people were able to resist Mewuya's evil powers. He could no longer hypnotize people to do his wishes. That no one was obeying him made Mewuya *veryvery* upset. He shouted and shouted, but none of the villagers came out.

"Then he got *reallyreally* upset. With his heart all spoiled with anger, he made a mad dash toward the first hut he saw. But Kantamanto, who was ready and standing by with his medicine, went into action."

Uwargida became a bit animated at this point. She opened her eyes widely and gesticulated with her weak arms. We, in turn, became less scared upon hearing that someone was at last putting up a fight to stop the little devil.

"The priest wore a long red-hooded gown that touched his

feet. The only visible parts of his body were his eyes, fingers, and his bare feet. In one hand he held a wooden staff and in the other he held a gourd filled with talismans for different magical commands. He balanced another gourd on his head, this one filled with potions used for various magical purposes only Allah knows. And as much as the priest turned, bent, or even ran, the gourd remained on his head, as if it was part of his body.

"Just as Mewuya was entering the door of the first hut, the fetish priest hit his staff against the ground and tilted his head to pour some of his powerful potion on the ground. A colorless vapor emerged from the ground, and instantly the universe turned completely dark, something that had never before been seen. Mewuya suddenly realized he couldn't see anything, not even his sword. And though he was not prepared for a challenge of that nature, he, too, began to work his magic. Kato and Mewuya fought and fought and fought in the dark for what seemed like an eternity to the villagers, who remained locked inside their huts, listening to the sharp and rumbling noises made by the clashing of their supernatural magic.

"Finally, Mewuya succeeded in breaking the old man's spell. With a single strike of his sword into the air, the boy reversed the priest's medicine, turning the darkness into a bright daylight, also something that had never before been seen.

"The old man engaged Mewuya in another long duel, at the end of which he changed the daylight to darkness again. The boy instantly reversed it. Again, the old man changed it to darkness. The boy created day. The fetish priest turned it into night. And it has been so ever since, and that's why we have day turning into night and night into day. The fetish priest and the boy are still out there in the firmament, dueling, until the day one of them defeats or kills the other. And that day, boys and girls, shall be the end of this our universe.

Uwargida paused briefly, and then concluded "the mother of all stories" with the meaningless phrase we always used at the end of a tale: *Khulungus kan gus.*

"This would've been a lie if it weren't for the sake of Mr. Spider," we chorused the familiar response before dispersing in a hurry to go to sleep in our mothers' rooms.

THE PROPHET OF ZONGO STREET

I was nine years old when I first met Kumi. He used to be one of our neighbors on Zongo Street, a densely populated section of Kumasi, Ghana's most prosperous city. Kumi was tall, lanky, handsome, and always well dressed: clean white shirt, black tie, and nearly pressed khaki trousers. He wore black shoes, and his strides were long and slow. His hair was nicely combed and he shaved every morning before he left home for the Central Post Office in the town proper, where he worked as a mail clerk.

Kumi lived by himself in an unadorned two-bedroom house that was located at the dead end of Zongo Street. A low bamboo fence surrounded the house, to keep pedestrians away. The fence was painted black, and so were the shutters of Kumi's building, but for reasons known only to himself, Kumi left the rest of the building unpainted. He was probably the only person on our side of the street who liked flowers; the hibiscus were his favorite, and he planted them all over his little compound.

Books were stacked everywhere inside Kumi's living room—

small books, large books, old books, and even antique manu-
scripts that were written entirely by hand. The windows of the
house were always shut, and the only source of light in his living
room was an old, rusty hurricane lantern that sat on his study
table. This always left the living room in half-darkness, which he
seemed to prefer. A large portrait of his children—two boys of
about the ages seven and nine—hung on the wall of Kumi's liv-
ing room, though he never talked about them. There was specu-
lation that his wife had tried for months to seek a divorce from
him without any success and that he had come back home from
work one afternoon to an empty house. She had run away, tak-
ing along their two sons. This had happened about two years be-
fore Kumi moved to Zongo Street, when he used to live in Ash
Town, another suburb of the city. Mansa BBC—the name we
gave our street's biggest gossip, a large, garrulous woman—
claimed that Kumi's wife had run away because she believed he
was mad. Of course no sane person on the street believed BBC's
story, as every aspect of Kumi's life seemed to reflect that of a full
gentleman. And besides that, Kumi had never been seen talking
aloud to himself or running around naked in the market square,
as some mad people in town did.

Though Kumi's reticence and shyness made him quite unap-
proachable, his generosity made him a favorite of many people
on Zongo Street. He seldom mixed with the people, and yet he
was respected by almost everyone: men and women, adults and
young children. His aloofness was not because he was Western-
educated and therefore considered himself better than the
streetfolks—a very common trait among such types on Zongo
Street and in the city. He was a person who humbly devoted

himself to his books and his "thoughts," even though he did care for other people, especially the children in and around our neighborhood. On the few occasions Kumi mingled with people on the street—when he attended burial ceremonies—he sat far away from the crowd, in a corner, surrounded by little children, who were his best friends.

Unlike his fellow adults who gathered at Aliko's barbershop to engage in idle chatter, which usually ended in heated arguments, Kumi never opened his mouth to quarrel with anyone. He frequented the barbershop as often as twice each week, but he went only to get his hair trimmed. Kumi was always seen with his face buried in either a book or a newspaper, as if avoiding the stares of people on the street. He would only lift his head whenever someone greeted him, and would only say: "How are you being treated by Fate?"

On Friday evenings he would invite me and my friends for a *biyan-tankwa* and biscuit party. And almost every day, on his way home from work, he bought for me, my brothers, and sisters presents of meat pies and Fanta drinks. My mother would thank Kumi when he brought the gifts to us, and at the same time she would ask him to stop buying such expensive food, insisting that it would spoil us.

At most of the weekly parties Kumi threw for me and my friends, he talked endlessly about the importance of education and the need to become good citizens of our community.

"You boys should take your studies seriously in order to become responsible adults in the future . . . you do not want to end up like Suraju," Kumi would say in his soft voice. Suraju was Zongo Street's most notorious swindler and petty thief; he was a drunkard as well. "All of you here know that Suraju would have led a decent life if he had had an education. It would have given him a decent job instead of the wretched life he is leading, sleeping all day long and getting up at night to steal and drink. Don't you agree with me?" Kumi would ask.

We would all reply yes, raising our fists in the air as if we really understood what he was talking about.

Kumi, at times, talked to us about Socrates, Nietzsche, Kant, and Spinoza. My friends and I had no idea who these people were—I didn't even know what the word *philosophy* meant at that time—but Kumi claimed that they were the greatest people who had ever lived and had tried, by means of their ideas, to re-create the world. He never explained to us why the ideas of these people failed. To be honest, Kumi's stories were quite boring at times, but we listened to them anyway—because of the food he gave us.

The more I went to Kumi's flat, the more curious I became about his life; and it was partly because I never knew exactly what mood he was in at any given time. His face had an expression that showed neither sadness nor happiness; it did not resemble any form of sentiment I knew. I wondered what he thought about when he was alone in his flat and happened not to be reading.

Once when my friends and I were visiting Kumi, I asked him:

"Are you happy?"

Even before the words were completely out of my mouth, I

realized how wrong it was of me, a mere child, to ask him such a question. At first I thought he would be upset and chide me, but in a friendly tone he asked: "Must one always be happy?"

I did not know what to say, and so I kept silent and looked away from him. For a while, Kumi did not say a word, either, and I realized that he was waiting for me to speak. My friends sat uneasily, with a drawn and embarrassed look on their faces.

After a brief silence, I stammered, "I . . . I thought every person wants to be happy all the time. I want to . . . I want to be happy all the time."

Kumi smiled. "Listen carefully, young man, and all of you here as well," he said. He moved his cane chair closer to where the four of us sat on the couch. "We human beings live every day of our lives in expectation of happiness." He paused, looked at me, and then continued. "But have you wondered why no son of Adam has ever attained complete happiness in his lifetime?" he asked, looking at us one by one.

We did not say a word. The truth was that we had nothing to say. We looked away from him and then at one another like a flock of sheep in a small, tight pen. I did not have any idea what my friends were thinking at the time, but personally, I was already regretting that I had started the whole thing. Moments passed without any of us responding to Kumi's question, and so he continued.

"The reason we are never happy in life is that we are never content with what we have. The only means by which one could attain complete happiness is to avoid living in constant expectation of it. It's the expectation that causes our unhappiness and consequent bitterness about life." I did not know exactly what

Kumi meant by that, but I went along with it all the same and nodded my head—as my friends did.

Kumi then began a long discourse that he concluded by saying, "Happiness is nothing but the comfort of illusion." *Happiness is nothing but the comfort of illusion?* I was hopelessly confused, and one of my friends was already dozing by the time Kumi reached this point in his lecture. Sensing our discomfort, Kumi quickly moved onto another topic—a topic on which he had often delivered long sermons to us.

"You must be able to restrict your utterances, young men, or else you and trouble will forever dwell together. You should always remember that we human beings are what we say. Many times, greatly respected people have lost their dignity in the eyes of other people because they have allowed their mouths to precede their minds. Our egos may reside in our minds, but it is the mouth that makes them known to the rest of the world. So be mindful of what you say."

My friends and I were exhausted after Kumi's long sermon. Before we left his house, he gave each one of us two toffees and encouraged us to visit again the next day.

During one of my numerous visits to Kumi, he told me that books are far better companions than human beings, because one learns from reading, and that unlike humans, books are reliable. Kumi spent his free time reading books that were as huge as the encyclopedias I saw in the Ashanti Library. He once told me that those books he read were books of theology. I didn't know what theology was, so I asked him what the books were really about. He told me that they were the lost books of Moses and all the Hebrew and Quraish apostles mentioned in the Bible and the Koran.

"Then how come you have them? Who gave these sacred books to you?"

"Don't worry, young man." he said, laughing. "This is beyond you now, but you'll understand later as you grow up."

As time went by, I gave up my attempts to understand Kumi, though I still visited his house quite regularly. And then one evening he told me something that confused me more than ever. I didn't know whether to believe him or not. He told me that the history of the world was somehow fabricated by the white man.

"They changed everything in the original book of scriptures and filled it with false dogmas that suited their own greedy intentions," he said.

He also told me that the black race would have dominion over the rest of the world before it ends; he even claimed to know exactly when the world was going to come to an end. I asked him how he found that out.

"It was predetermined," he replied. "The supreme ruler of the universe, in his revelation to Moses, predicted all of these and many other hidden truths, but they were altered."

"By who?"

Kumi replied harshly: "Didn't you hear me? I said the white man!" Such harshness was quite unusual for him. He shoved a huge book in front of my face and asked me to read and find out for myself. Scared, I quickly left, forgetting to take the book with me.

Later that day, after the evening meal, I told my mother

about what Kumi had said to me, though I failed to mention his harsh attitude toward me. She said: "Do not go to his house so much. That man does not look healthy to me these days. He seems to be crazy in the head."

I silently disagreed with my mother, and I was, for a while, upset with her for speaking the way she did about my friend, though the dramatic change in him was evident. He stopped inviting us for drinks and biscuits on Friday nights, and also refrained from delivering presents to me and my sister. He no longer seemed to care so much about his neat appearance and demeanor. My friends rarely visited his house by this time. The neatly stacked books in his living room were now scattered everywhere, making it difficult for one to find space even to put one's feet. His hibiscus flowers began to wilt and died in the end. But despite all this, nothing Mother said about him was enough to deter me from going to see Kumi, who after nearly four years of friendship had become one of the most important people in my life. I always came up with new excuses that would get me out of our house so that I could visit him. I would tell Mother that one of my friends had borrowed my textbook at school and that I was going to collect it. Before leaving our house, I would throw one of my books out the window, so that I could carry it back inside with me, after I had visited Kumi.

On one of these visits, Kumi looked me in the eye and said: "I am beginning a serious study of the history of mankind, and so I want you to stop coming here. I'll let you know when I am finished with my studies, so that you can start visiting again." He then rapped his fingers on my head. He also gave me a little book that was entitled *Manifestations* and urged me to read it as soon as I could. I tried to read the book upon returning home that evening, putting aside my homework, but couldn't understand most of what I read. It was not until several weeks later—after reading and rereading many sections of the book—that I finally began to get a grasp of its contents. It was written in 1932 by one Anthony Mtoli, a self-proclaimed "Africanist" and "Spiritualist" whom I had never heard of before. The book called for a universal black rebellion against "white dominance," and was full of curses and diatribes on Europeans, Arabs, and all white-skinned people. It was shocking and scary. I was brought up not only to revere Arabs and their culture, but to see each of them as a paragon of beauty, virtue, and spirituality. Islam was my religion, and Islam's prophet was himself Arab. At the madrassa, or Islamic school, I was led to believe that all white people were geniuses and daredevils, and that Arabs were divine among humans. And there I was, reading that some "Arab Invaders" had once waged wars against black people in West Africa, and in the process of that war, had enslaved my ancestors and forced them to convert to Islam. For the first time I realized that there actually was a period in history when the people of my tribe, Hausa, weren't Muslims at all. Before I read *Manifestations*, I never doubted that humanity itself began with Islam, and that God had chosen a prohet among the Arabs because they were morally and spiritually superior to the rest of humankind.

Night after night, before I went to sleep, I read and reread *Manifestations*. I was thirteen at the time, and the more I understood the book's contents, the more I thought about Kumi and wondered what he might be doing at that time. I was afraid to share my findings in the book with anyone, and eagerly awaited the day Kumi would again invite me to his house; I longed to impress him with my knowledge of the book he had given me. But my hope and excitement amounted to nothing. Fate had it that I was never to see the inside of Kumi's house again.

During the first two months Kumi barred me from his flat, it was obvious that something was really bothering him, though no one could tell what it was. He walked hurriedly now, whispering to himself all the time, with no paper or book held to his face. He hardly responded to people's greetings anymore, including Mother's. As time went by, he was seldom seen on the street. I guessed he had stopped working at the post office as well, because one of his coworkers came to our house to inquire about his continued absence.

One night, some six weeks after Kumi was last seen, we heard loud, piercing noises coming from his house. And each night after that the noises grew louder and more intense. People began to gather in front of the building at night to listen, although no one understood what the noises meant or what was actually going on inside. Rumor had it that the noises were made by the ghost of an old man who, many years ago, was buried on the plot where Kumi's building was erected. The noises sounded like the voices of a thousand people, all of them chanting, screaming, and shrieking. At one point, the street's imam gave an order that any person who valued his life should not go near the house at night. As soon as it became dark, parents locked their children inside for fear of the bad spirits believed to be hidden in Kumi's bedroom. Even the adults, when they walked near his house, did so in quick strides, as if they were being pursued.

The people on the street wished they could ignore the horrible noises, but it was impossible; they continued to get louder and more intense with the passing of each night. Meanwhile another rumor spread that Kumi had gone insane because he had read too many books. Yet another rumor suggested that he had died, and that the noises were made by *his* ghost.

Then early one Friday morning—roughly three weeks after the noises had begun—we heard Kumi shouting. A handful of people came out to see what was the matter with him. They saw Kumi pacing up and down the street, holding a huge book, from which he recited. His normally clean-shaven face was now heavily bearded and his hair was curled into short, thick dreadlocks. Kumi had grown very skinny, almost skeletal. He was barefoot and was clad in a long white robe, with a red cotton belt tied around his thin waist.

Later that day, in the afternoon, people flocked into our neighborhood to listen to Kumi's sermons. For a while he was entertaining. He danced and chanted in praise of Ti-gari, whom Kumi claimed was the "supreme ruler of the universe." Kumi made gestures, shrieked, and stamped his feet on the ground in his spiritual delight.

"I am only a messenger," he cried. "For hundreds of years you people have been led astray. You have been made to bow down to the images of false prophets and abstract gods, thinking that you are bowing down to the supreme ruler of the universe, Ti-gari himself. Look around you here. Look at the poverty in which you live; look at the misery, the ignorance, the disease. And yet you continue to worship their so-called omnipotent and beneficent Gods . . . The Christian slave traders told you that Jesus is the son of God, and this Jesus, according to them, is white. Meanwhile, the Islamic Invaders had already arrived and told our ancestors that it is because of the love of only one human being by the name of Muhammad that the world itself was created. You must remember that this Muhammad is supposedly white too, a white Arab."

Kumi claimed that everything he preached was revealed to him by the god of his new religion in nightly visions. It drove me close to tears when I stood among my junior secondary school mates and watched as he raved. I tried to talk to him at the end of his first preaching session, but he acted as if I were a complete stranger. That night I cried silently before I went to sleep, careful not to let my mother hear.

"Long before these invaders came to our land, we had our own gods, gods of our ancestor's ancestors. We also had Ti-gari, who ruled over all the gods and men in this universe. Unlike the abstract and partial gods brought to us by these invaders, Ti-gari and the gods of our ancestors are merciful, generous, and sympathetic to the needs of people of all races—ours especially. Our ancestors used to live with these gods, and with Ti-gari himself. They talked face-to-face with the supreme ruler in their shrines, and all their needs were fulfilled. And then came the Muslims and Christians with their gods! What did our ancestors do? They quickly abandoned their God, not knowing that these invaders had come to them with scriptures in one hand and a sword or chain hidden in the other, ready to capture and take them away. The Christian and Islamic intrusionists came and asked our ancestors to look up into the sky, to look up to Heaven, while they filled their ships with our gold, young men and women, timber, diamonds, cocoa—the list is endless. And even to this very day, we continue to allow them to strip us of our rightful and natural possessions that have been bequeathed to us by Ti-gari. Why can't we see the foolery? Why can't we see the betrayal? Why do we continue to take this insult? Why?" Kumi at times seemed to lack answers for some of his own profound questions.

People turned out in great numbers during the early days of his preaching. And while some of them were inclined to believe in Kumi's new religion, others thought he had gone mad or that his behavior was the result of heavy drinking.

"According to the scriptures they brought to you, Jesus is said to have hair like lamb's wool," Kumi shouted during an afternoon of preaching. "Now, you all know what a lamb's wool looks like. Just like your hair and my hair, right? Why then? Why didn't we question the Europeans when they brought us the blond-haired and blue-eyed pictures of Jesus, telling us that he is the son of their God? And why didn't we question the Arabs, who bought and sold our ancestors into slavery, while preaching to us that their religion is one of peace and equality? Because you know what, Brothers and Sisters? It was because we allowed our minds to be carried away by false promises of gold, wicked glory, and an eternal redemption that is nothing but a hoax!"

Kumi knelt down at this point, and from his bag he pulled out a portrait of a man he claimed to be the real Jesus, and whose true name according to him was I'sama. He raised up the portrait—which was drawn on a large piece of cardboard—so that everyone present could see. The figure in the portrait had overgrown bushy hair, a flat nose, prominent lips, and dark skin. He returned the portrait to his bag after a short while, and then continued with his preaching. "And so, Brothers and Sisters, do not bow down to any false images of I'sama. He is a servant of Ti-gari and not a son of any of their gods, as they made you to believe. And remember always that he is as black as anyone among you here."

I did not know what to think of Kumi's new religion, which he called Afromadiya. I asked my mother's opinion about it, and all she said to me was, "Too much knowledge at times leads people to the ways of the devil." She then warned me to stay completely away from Kumi. Part of me began to think that he might actually be evil. And yet another part of me refused to believe all the speculation that went on about him, and I argued with schoolmates of mine who believed him mad.

In her bid to console me about Kumi's plight, Mother told me that people who were crazy had the same capacity to create justifications for their behavior as normal people did. I realized that her explanation—as rational as it seemed—was probably intended to make me understand how hopeless Kumi's situation was, and thereby help me to come to terms with it. Her attempt, however, had the opposite effect on me: I developed an even greater feeling of pity for Kumi, saying to myself that he was a victim of a power or force I did not know.

Then things began to get worse for poor Kumi. His body began to smell; he had apparently stopped taking baths. He was obviously not eating, as he grew thinner and thinner. Some of the kinder people on the street, including a few of his relatives who lived on Zerikyi Road, tried to talk Kumi out of his new occupation, but he refused to listen to anyone. Some even attempted to send him to the mental asylum in the town proper, but he cursed and threatened them, saying that whoever touched him would be afflicted with an incurable disease. In the end, he was left alone.

Despite Kumi's deteriorating health, he still remained unrelenting in his attempt to spread the new religion. And by this time, seven months into his vocation as a preacher, everyone on the street had lost interest in listening to what Kumi had to say, with the exception of the children, who took him as a mere entertainer. After a while, however, even the children got tired of listening to Kumi's exhortations. But that did not discourage him from preaching, which he did day and night, rain or shine. Gradually, his voice grew thin, almost inaudible. People began to walk past him without even looking at him. He meanwhile remained the only known convert to this new religion.

Then one day during the rainy season, there came a terrible storm. The wind that followed the rain ripped off the roofs of many buildings on Zongo Street. It rained continuously for three days and nights, with thunder and lightning, as if the whole world was coming to an end. During this storm, while people were in their houses—praying for the protection of their lives and property—Kumi was outside preaching to no one but himself. We would peep through our windows to see him pacing up and down the muddied street, still preaching, his voice drowned out by the pounding rain.

After this fateful storm Kumi was not seen on the street for a couple of days. I had a feeling that some terrible thing had happened to him, but I had no idea what it might be. Two nights after the storm, I had a dream, and in that dream I saw Kumi being lifted up into the sky by black angels. I told my mother about this dream the following morning, but she hushed me up and warned me not to disclose "this ominous dream" to anyone, not even to my father.

On the third day after the storm, while people were still trying to repair their damaged roofs and fences, some concerned neighbors decided to find out what had happened to Kumi. These neighbors, including my father, knocked several times on Kumi's door, but heard no response. A day was allowed to pass, in the hope that he would come out if he was in the building, but this hope ended in vain.

Five days passed, and Kumi was still not seen. And since attempts to contact Kumi's family had proved futile—they didn't want to have anything to do with him—the street's elders then decided that his house must be broken into. It did not take my father and the others much effort to break into the building, because they found the main door unlocked. They pushed it open and walked inside. Kumi was found lying on his bed, pale and quite dead. He was still clad in his white robe, and the red cotton belt was tied tightly around his thin waist. And out on the street people whispered darkly that a book, a very large one, lay open on his chest.

Everything about Kumi's funeral was carried out hastily. Instead of the three to seven days that were usually spent mourning and praying for the dead, not even a full day was spent for him. And not many people attended the funeral either, not even his runaway wife and two children. A handful of his friends from the post office and about a dozen people from the street made up the entire gathering at the ceremony; and they could barely wait for the imam's closing prayers, so that they could leave and attend to their personal affairs.

Parents on the street forbade their children to go near the place where Kumi's funeral was being held, claiming that his ominous death might bring ill luck to their families. But despite this fear, my father took me along with him. I sat on a short stool the whole time the prayers were being recited, with my mind not on the imam's words but on the book that Kumi had given to me, the little book that had not only revealed to me the highest truth about humanity but had also taught me things I never before knew about myself, my family, clan, tribe, and race. I wondered if my father had ever read such a book, and what his thoughts might have been about it. But I dared not ask Father questions like that—a fourteen-year-old like me wasn't supposed to ask questions anyway, especially if those questions raised doubts about Islam and any of our traditions. So I walked silently behind my father after the prayers, anxious to reach home so that I could read aloud, as a memorial, passages from *Manifestations*, which was at that time tucked in between the skin of my belly and the waistband of my khaki shorts.

LIVE-IN

"The money," Shatu blurts out. "I can't find it." She opens her palms and lifts both hands in the air, as if she expects the money to drop on the floor. She recalls it being in her left hand just a short while ago. Or it was my right hand? she wonders. She pats her breast, pokes a finger in her bodice, and searches all her pockets. She finds the crumpled shopping list, but not the grocery money Marge Hammers, the woman Shatu works for as a live-in maid, has given her just a short while ago. As chilled as the fully air-conditioned supermarket is, Shatu feels sweat oozing all over her body. "Maybe I accidentally dropped it in one of the aisles," she says in a childish and agonized tone.

The cashier at register four, whose brightly lettered pink-and-white name tag identifies her as Tammy, stares at Shatu through thick prescription glasses, her eyes blue and vibrant. Robust-looking and auburn-haired, Tammy is in her mid-forties and a single mother of three, two boys and a girl. She is also an avid churchgoer and a hard worker whose cheerfulness and courtesy to customers has won her several "Employee of the Month" awards during her nine years of employment at the Emporium Supermarket.

"Why don't you go look for it," says Tammy, her freckled face retaining its bright smile. "Don't worry, I'll hold up the cash register."

As Shatu makes her way back to the aisles, the cashier turns and says to the customers behind Shatu, "Sorry, folks, do you mind moving to the next register, the one over here." She points to a cashier two registers away. Like truck drivers who must back up from the scene of an accident, the three middle-aged housewives pull their shopping carts in reverse order and then, in a forward motion, steer toward the empty register.

Shatu runs from aisle to aisle, panting heavily. She feels a sharp pain in her chest, a pain that has become frequent of late. Shatu is afraid of what Marge will say when she hears about the lost money. She is also concerned about not disturbing the peace of the rich white shoppers in the supermarket with her black histrionics, and most important, about making the housewives feel insecure in her presence. Calm your heart. Control yourself, she admonishes herself, and quickly slows her pace.

Shatu combs through every aisle, including the organic food section, a part of the supermarket she almost never visits. After fifteen minutes of continued searching, there is still no sign of the money. Shatu retreats to the checkout area.

"You can't find it?" Tammy asks when Shatu returns. Shatu opens her mouth and makes an attempt to speak, but instead tears run down her cheeks. Almost immediately her eyes turn red and swollen. Two impeccably dressed women from the next aisle walk over to see if she's all right. Shatu doesn't know the names of the women, though she sees them often at the supermarket, and has exchanged nods and hellos with them on several occasions. The women pat Shatu on the back, offering half-hearted consolations, as if it were required of them, and then go back to their own carts. Other customers simply sneer at Shatu and walk past.

"Don't cry, hon," says Tammy. "Someone might find it, you know."

Shatu tilts her head downward, then masks her face in a fake smile, one she struggles to maintain every day in the face of white people.

Tammy then grabs the microphone next to her and turns on the switch. "Good afternoon, shoppers. A lady has just reported the loss of two hundred dollars in the store. If you find this money, please return it to the customer-service desk at the back of the store."

"In what denominations is the amount, hon?" Tammy asks Shatu.

"Huh?" Shatu asks in return.

"The bills, notes, are they in twenty-dollar bills, fifty-dollar bills, hundred?" asks the cashier.

"Oh, sorry, twenty, twenty. Ten twenty," replies Shatu, sneezing.

"The money is in twenty-dollar bills. Thank you," adds Tammy over the crisp loudspeaker system. Shatu wonders if this detail will at all be the deciding factor.

With her usual politeness, Tammy asks Shatu to remove her shopping items from the conveyor belt and to step aside. The cashier presses a combination of buttons on the cash register, which in turn produces a series of ticking sounds, to cancel Shatu's bill. Shatu then begins the tedious task of reloading the cart with Ritz crackers; white rice; pepperoni; Dole apple sauce; fresh meat and fish; Tide detergent; White Castle micowaveable cheeseburgers; potato chips; toilet rolls; Prima Familia Italian Style meatballs—also microwaveable; adult diapers; fresh ginger; Tyson's ready-to-fry chicken breast nuggets; canned soups; generic frozen TV lunches and dinners; frozen pizza; microwaveable popcorn; and Clorox bleach.

"Next customer, please," Tammy calls while waving at an elderly man, who is accompanied by a young Eastern European–looking maid. Shatu has seen the duo many times at the supermarket, and each time she sees them it never ceases to amaze her that there are white people who do the same kind of work she does.

Shatu arrived in New York City a year ago at the invitation of Rakiya, her older sister who lived in the Bronx with her two children (a boy and a girl) and Yellow Cab driver husband, who was also from Shatu's town of Kumasi, in Ghana. Due to lack of good record-keeping on the part of her parents, Shatu didn't know her real age. So, when she was confronted with the need to secure the passport for her trip to the United States, Shatu compared and contrasted and added and subtracted the ages of her childhood friends, and finally arrived at the approximate conclusion that she was born anywhere between 1962 and 1964. She declared the arbitrary date of August 3, 1963, as her birthday, pegging her age at thirty-seven.

Back in Ghana, Shatu was hardly making ends meet. Her husband, Dan Kwairo, had died only two years before her trip to the United States, and didn't leave behind any money or property. She and her three children (a boy of sixteen, and two girls, ages fourteen and eleven) were evicted from the house they lived in, as she couldn't afford the rent. Shatu and her children had then moved back to her mother's family house on Zongo Street, where she and her orphaned children joined the company of the fifty-people-strong extended family that lived in the compound. Although Rakiya had remitted Shatu and their mother a hundred dollars at the end of each month, it just wasn't enough to cater for the five of them. And they didn't receive any help from Shatu's father, who divorced her mother when Shatu was fourteen, and moved to a town in the south, where he remarried and started a new family.

Well versed in the ways and means of the underground immigrant community in the Bronx, Rakiya used her own green card and landed Shatu a job as a live-in maid. It was the job of choice for most Ghanaian immigrants, because, decent salary aside, they saved more of their income due to the free room and board that comes with such employment. Initially Shatu was a little skeptical and actually quite afraid of moving in with someone she had never met before, given especially that the person was white. Before her arrival in the United States, Shatu had barely seen white people on Zongo Street, let alone spoken to one. But Rakiya, who had been living in the United States for nine years and was slightly Americanized in her mannerisms, had quelled Shatu's apprehension, saying, "They are not going to eat you up, and trust me, such things are not going to matter to you once you hold some dollars in between your fingers." Shatu did not argue with her sister; she knew the value of a dollar all too well. When converted into cedis, the Ghanaian currency, a dollar was capable of feeding an adult for a day, and sumptuously so—including soft drinks and iced water, the consumption of which symbolized "good living" among the local folks. Before long, Shatu was enjoying the American opulence she had often heard about from her sister—the abundance of food, clothing, jewelry, and perfume; the twenty-four-hour television programming and the hundreds of channels to choose from; and the new sense of dignity she had felt ever since she arrived in New York. Still, Shatu never forgot her children and mother, to whom she wasted no time in sending some money as soon as she had received her first paycheck.

Shatu was hired as Marge Hammers's live-in maid during the spring of the new millennium. Two weeks earlier, Marge, a cranky, paranoid, and senile woman of seventy-eight, had fallen in front of her Long Island house, and had rolled down the sloping lawn of her property all the way to the curb. After the accident, Marge's physician at Huntington Hospital insisted that the old woman receive twenty-four-hour care at home. Previously Marge had refused all attempts made by her nephew, Roger, and also by her financial planner-cum-procurement manager, Alison Price, to secure a permanent caretaker; Marge had insisted that she was capable of managing on her own. She only allowed the services of a freelance maid, who came in biweekly to clean the house, refill her medications at the pharmacy, and buy her groceries.

Roger is Marge's only known relative and the only person she really listens to. He is in his late forties and is, as far as Shatu knows, on a disability allowance of some sort, so he longer works. Like his aunt, Roger is a loner who lives in the Midwestern town of Akron, Ohio, where he lives by himself in a three-bedroom house from which he remotely conducts the affairs of his old aunt by telephone. As her legal custodian, Roger is responsible for Marge's overall well-being, and must approve every decision that affects her physical and medical upkeep. Although he never visits her, he calls her almost every day of the week. And their conversations, boring as they are, seem to lessen the loneliness of their lives.

Though Shatu's agent and actual employer, Home Comfort Care, or H.C.C, had already screened, interviewed, and assigned her to Marge, Roger had demanded to interview her himself before she began working for his aunt; he insisted that his aunt would throw a fit if she later discovered that he hadn't personally screened the maid.

"Where are you from, originally?" Roger had asked Shatu during the telephone interview.

"I am from Ghana," Shatu had said.

"O, Guy-*anna*, beautiful. I like your sweet Caribbean accent, Sha-tu."

Shatu giggled, and mindful of her people's adage to be cautious and respectful when one finds his fingers in a lion's mouth, Shatu thought it prudent not to correct his misguided perception of her "Caribbeanness."

Roger was taken by Shatu's docility, the way she punctuated her answers with "yes, sir," "no, sir," and "thank you, sir." Her affable phone manners and courtesy made him feel a sense of loss for something he couldn't quite pin down. Less than ten minutes into the interview, which had quickly turned into mere chitchat, Roger had said to Shatu, "I am very delighted to hire you to work for my aunt." He sounded exuberant, as if Shatu was the one doing him a favor.

"Thank you, sir. Thank you," Shatu repeated, scarcely believing her good luck.

"Not a problem. Let me know if you need anything," Roger had told the ecstatic Shatu.

She moved in with Marge the following day.

Marge was bedridden during the first few weeks of Shatu's employment—the result of a broken hip and a lacerated shoulder she suffered from her fall. Shatu fed, bathed, dressed, and catered to Marge's every need and urge. She held the potty while Marge relieved herself. Then she placed the bedpan on the floor, wiped Marge clean, and fit her with a new diaper. Though Shatu was dismayed by most of what her job required her to do—which included suffering through Marge's wild mood swings and unkindness—she thought it cruel that Marge, at her advanced age, didn't have any blood relative nearby to care for her.

Marge's circumstances made Shatu think about her own grandmother, who was well into her eighties, and lived in quite an enviable state compared to Marge. In these final years of her long life, Shatu's grandmother had become the repository of the community's age-old wisdom and knowledge; people who wished to be the beneficiaries of her wise counsel and blessing flocked to her day and night. In the evenings she was surrounded by her many grandchildren, who begged her to tell them Mallam Gizo, or Mr. Spider tales. But here, Shatu mused, old people are forsaken by their own blood, and are left to die in the hands of strangers.

Despite Marge's mood swings and mean attitude, all of which Shatu attributed to loneliness—Marge's husband had died some thirty years ago and they had no children—and the effect of the dozens of drugs Marge took daily, Shatu still managed to be kind and gentle toward her mistress. But almost as soon as Marge had regained her health, she demanded that Roger fire Shatu.

That night Roger called Shatu. "I am sorry about the way my aunt has treated you. You don't deserve that at all," Roger said.

"Thank you, sir. Thank you. I was thinking to myself, what did I do to this woman? After all that I have done for her these past two months . . ."

"I know, Sha-tu, you don't have to tell me. You've been excellent! Listen, she can't fire you, I am . . ."

Roger stopped in midsentence, and asked, "Are you there, Sha-tu?"

"Hmm, yes, sir, I am here."

"I said don't worry at all about your job. My aunt was just being silly, but she knows how good and important you are to her well-being."

"Thank you, sir, but sometimes I worry about my future, because human beings are not so predictable."

"Sha-tu," said Roger, laughing. "I have told you not to worry, she is just being hysterical. Just ignore her."

Shatu heaved a sigh of relief, and then sniffled.

"As a matter of fact, Sha-tu, Marge and I have decided to reward you with a gift for all your hard work these past weeks."

"Oh, thank you sir, you don't have to . . ."

"Now, tell me. Is there anything in particular you want?" Roger asked. "Pick whatever you like, and I will pay for it."

"Oh, thank you, sir," Shatu said, baffled by the surprise generosity. "As for me, I am happy here, but if you buy me a TV for my room I will be grateful."

"Is that it? You don't want chains, a bracelet or anything?" asked Roger, who had begun to sound quite animated and jovial.

"No, the TV is enough, sir. Thank you and God bless you."

The next afternoon Alison dropped off a brand-new twenty-inch color television, a Toshiba with a built-in VCR player. Alison then informed Shatu to clear a corner of her room, as people from the local phone company were coming over the next day to install a new line in Shatu's room. Though Shatu didn't ask for a private phone, she took it to be part of the guilt-inspired generosity from her employers. Still, she thanked them profusely for "all that you have done for me."

That night Roger called Shatu on the private line.

"So, you like your new phone?" he had asked after the initial greetings.

"Yes, thank you, sir."

"You're welcome. Is there anything else you want?

"No, sir, I am fine, thank you."

"All right, just let me know if anything bothers you over there, okay?

"Okay, sir."

Roger had said good-bye and hung up the phone, only to call back five minutes later.

"Hello, Sha-tu, it's me again. I am just calling to tell you I like listening to your voice."

"Oh, thank you, sir."

"And I also want you to know that you can pick up the phone and call me anytime you want to chat."

"Okay, sir," Shatu had replied stiffly, not knowing what to make of, first, Roger's compliment, and second, his gesture.

"Let me ask you a quick question if you don't mind," Roger had asked, just as she had hoped he was going to hang up.

"Okay."

"Are you married?"

"No, sir, my husband died."

"Sorry to hear that, Sha-tu."

Shatu was suddenly quiet, taken aback by Roger's question.

"Sha-tu, are you there?"

"Oh, yes, sir."

"Sorry to bother you."

"No problem."

Shatu went to sleep quite perturbed. She had heard stories of live-in maids being paid hundreds of dollars to perform sexual acts with their sickly, old male patients. Shatu suddenly felt nauseated. The mere thought of having an affair with Roger created a knot in her chest. She had pictured him as a wrinkly, fat man who, just like his aunt, was sickly and lonely and spent his days and nights watching TV and scratching his body.

Her little chat with Roger had opened an old wound—the devastation she had suffered after the death of her husband—and exposed Shatu to a new wound altogether, that of her actual unmarried status and the loneliness that went along with it. Shatu wondered if she would ever find another man to marry. Not if I remain holed up in this house, she thought.

A few nights later Roger called again, and soon afterward he took to calling Shatu frequently in the middle of the night, when she was either half-asleep or dozing in front of the television. He engaged her in long and winding conversations that had neither head nor tail. And even though Shatu didn't particularly enjoy Roger's conversations—and was certainly not interested in him—she picked up the phone so as not to appear rude to her employer. Roger would go on and on, asking her all sorts of questions about her life and even asking her how she looked.

"Where are you?" he once asked Shatu.

"In my room," Shatu answered.

"I know, I mean, where are you in your room? On your bed?" Though she was offended by Roger's question, Shatu still answered "yes," and asked him politely, "But why did you want to know where I am?"

"Nothing, just wondering," Roger said, laughing. That night, too, Shatu went to sleep in a disturbed mood, cursing the new phone line, wishing she could have it disconnected.

Shatu called her sister to talk to her about her problems with Roger and her general dissatisfaction with life, but her sister, who juggled a nursing job, the care of her two teenagers, and the duties of a traditional African wife—including all the shopping, cooking, and cleaning—often didn't have much time to speak on the phone. The sisters thus spoke briefly only a few times a month, not any more than they used to when Shatu was in Ghana.

"You don't see your family, you don't see any friends, all you do is work, work, work," Shatu had complained to her sister during a phone conversation. By now she had begun to feel that the sacrifice one had to make in order to make money in America was too much.

"That's how it is in this country," Rakiya had said. "I don't like it, either, and wished we could all move back home and leave behind all the backbreaking work we do, but you and I know the situation back home."

Once a month, Shatu took off all the three days she was allowed in a four-week period (during which H.C.C. hired a temporary maid for Marge), to spend time with her sister and nephews, to mingle with the thousands of Ghanaians who lived in the Bronx, and to buy some rare African food products she couldn't find on Long Island. On many such visits, Shatu contemplated telling Rakiya about Roger and about the unpleasantness of her job, but she feared that she might appear a whiner to her sister, or even worse, seem ungrateful for "what Allah has given her." Shatu, therefore, decided to internalize her fear, though it was eating her up day by day, and to pray to Allah to soothe her heart. But when the time came for her to return to Long Island, a place she could only think of as a necessary evil in her life, Shatu was filled with the utmost sadness and a renewed fear of the loneliness that awaited her.

An hour after Tammy's announcement, Shatu remains at the back of the checkout counter, sobbing intermittently, mumbling woebegone, incoherent singsong phrases in her native Hausa tongue. Ever since she came to work for Marge, Shatu has comported herself, especially in public, as if striving to be the goodwill ambassador of the hundreds of live-in maids—mainly Caribbeans and African blacks—who serve the rich and the affluent in the lily-white enclave of Southampton in Suffolk County, Long Island. But as much as she tries on this day, she is unable to carry herself in her usual dignified manner. Tammy, attending to the long line of customers in front of her register, is beginning to lose patience with Shatu. "Hon, I think you better stop crying. Go home and tell Marge what happened. I'm sure she'll understand, you know."

Shatu wants to tell Tammy that the lost money is not the only reason she is crying. She feels weak and vulnerable. This crippling feeling is made even worse by Shatu's limited English and the general lack of confidence that has dogged her all her adult life. A mixture of gas, water, and bile from her stomach rise painfully in her chest, and before she can do anything to stop it, it has already reached her throat. She makes a dash toward the electronic glass doors, bends her head near the triangular patch of green in front of the building, and vomits out her brunch— undigested chunks of rice balls and meat and a thin yellowy liquid from the peanut-butter soup.

On reaching the house, Shatu waits a few minutes in front of the door, imagining the possible consequences of her impending disclosure. She is almost two hours late now, and knows for sure that Marge is probably fuming with rage that she has taken so long to return. Marge is watching a soap opera when Shatu walks into the living room, and even though she is aware of the maid's presence, she continues staring at the screen. Not until Shatu is standing within three feet of her does Marge turn to look at her maid. As the two make eye contact, Shatu breaks down in tears, and it is with much effort that she is able to control herself and to tell Marge what has happened. Marge listens attentively, without any trace of anger or disappointment on her face.

A few moments later, Marge asks Shatu for her walking aid, a Folding Walker brand she uses for mobility around the house. Slowly but surely, Old Marge walks the twelve steps or so to her bedroom, which usually takes her about four minutes. She emerges from the room with two crisp hundred-dollar bills, which she hands to Shatu, without comment. Shatu is not quite sure what to make of her mistress's kindness, but nevertheless is able to say in between sobs, "Thank you very much, madam. May God bless you."

"Don't be silly," Marge replies.

Shatu's grandmother had narrated a tale to her when she was growing up. It was the tale of Mother Hen and her six young chicks, who lived once upon a time during an era of severe famine on the earth. At the beginning of each month, the mother would send the chicks into the wilderness to find food for the family. On their return from their first successful hunt, Mother Hen, even before touching the food, asked her children where they had found it and also, most important, how the owner had reacted when they had taken the food. The chicks, it seems, had no option but to steal, as the farms and wilderness were completely scraped of every available grain. They explained to their mother that they had stolen the food from a gorilla family and that the entire monkey clan had given them chase for many miles, screaming at the top of their lungs, waving sticks and clubs in the air and even threatening to cut off their *chicken-heads* if they didn't return the food. After listening patiently to the story, Mother Hen had told her young ones, "Let's sit down and eat the food."

During their next foray, the chicks stole from a family of leopards, and the pack's reaction was similar to the monkey clan's; and the mother had once again asked her family to sit down and enjoy the food.

However, on the third adventure, the chicks stole from a fox pack that did not chase the culprits, but rather stood and watched as the chicks made away with their loot. When Mother Hen heard about the foxes' reaction, she asked her children to return the food to its owners, and proceeded to caution her young ones thus: The first two families expressed all their anger, frustration, and ill intentions just when you stole their food, and because of that, may have even forgotten about the theft soon after you had left. But beware of the person who hides his anger in his heart, for he may be planning a wicked revenge against you."

It amazes Shatu how relevant she still finds the morals of folk tales; the story is already making Shatu question Marge's generosity. Did she indeed give me the new two hundred dollars in good conscience or did she do so only to turn around and make me pay for it later? she wonders. "God save me," prays Shatu, as she walks past the automatic doors and into the cool interior of the supermarket.

One look at Tammy's disappointed face tells Shatu that the two hundred dollars have not been found.

"Sorry, hon, I made three more announcements since you left, but nothing so far."

"Okay, no problem. Everything is the work of God," says Shatu.

"We'll call Marge and let you guys know if someone finds it."

"Okay, no problem," Shatu says again, her eyes wandering around the checkout area, looking for her cart.

"Sorry, hon, but the floor guy restocked your cart. I wasn't sure if you were coming back or not," Tammy says and quickly returns to her customers.

Though she feels immense pain in both her stomach and chest, Shatu camouflages it with a grin. She fishes in her pocket for the shopping list, which is mercilessly crumpled. She turns and grabs a new shopping cart and quietly proceeds to the frozen food section, where she begins her shopping trip again.

It is sunset by the time Shatu returns with the groceries. Alison's car is in the driveway. Alison? ponders Shatu. Heavens, what is she doing here at this time of the day?

As Shatu pushes open the unlocked door, she overhears Marge saying, "I can do everything on my own. I don't need to pay her fifteen dollars an hour to live in my house and then steal my money. I want her fired!"

"No, Marge, I've told you this a dozen times before; we simply can't do that, okay?"

Leaving the door ajar, Shatu retreats in her steps and stands in front of the door listening to the two women.

"I want her out of my house. I can't live with a thief," Marge insists.

"Marge, stop it now, stop it! You are being ridiculous."

"It's my house and I cannot live with her," Marge yells.

"How many times do I need to tell you, we can't fire her. We need her. You need her. In case you have forgotten, the doctor still insists you have full-time care. You may think you are paying her too much, but the poor woman gets only half of the fifteen dollars we are being billed an hour. The rest goes to H.C.C. You should be thankful and grateful to her for doing the work she does for this kind of money." Alison seems truly upset, her voice growing louder and more animated with each syllable.

Marge bursts out crying.

Shatu opens the door and walks in, pulling behind her the four-wheel cart she takes with her to the supermarket. She proceeds, as noiselessly as she possibly can, to the kitchen.

Alison is now on the phone. She looks toward the kitchen door and nods at Shatu.

"Yes, it's me," Shatu hears Alison say. Then Alison begins to explain the case of the missing two hundred dollars. For the next five minutes, Shatu is forced to relive her afternoon, explained impassively by Alison to someone on the other line, presumably Roger. Every thirty seconds or so Alison is cut off, or answers a question, or goes silent. Meanwhile Marge is crying in the background. Shatu sits in a crouch on the kitchen's linoleum floor, listening as all this unfolds. "If only the earth will open its mouth and swallow me up right at this moment," Shatu whispers. "It would be preferable to this torture."

Fifteen minutes later, all is quiet in the house. Shatu is sitting in the chair in her room. Alison is at the door, on her way out. The phone rings in Shatu's room. She picks up the receiver to hear Roger's voice.

"Listen, I am so sorry about what happened," he says.

"I didn't know what happened, the money was in . . ."

"Sha-tu, I am not talking about the money. I am talking about my aunt's behavior. I am sorry about that. Please do me a favor; don't let her get to you," Roger says, in a soothing voice.

"Okay, thank you, sir," Shatu says, sobbing and smiling at the same time.

"Nothing will happen to your job, okay? Is there anything else you need?"

"No, nothing, sir. All I need is my job," she says, wiping her tears and drippy nose with the hem of her XX-large T-shirt.

"No problem, Sha-tu. Just let me know if you need anything else, okay?"

Shatu nods, sniffing.

"May God bless you," she says.

"Listen, you go back to your work. I'll call you later tonight or maybe tomorrow night, okay?"

"Sure. Thank you, sir."

At seven o'clock Shatu has finished all her evening chores. Old Marge, who seems to have forgotten about what happened that afternoon, is in her room, watching television as usual and munching on Jell-O pudding and thin crackers.

Shatu eats her dinner of jollof rice and gingered red snapper sauce in the silence of the kitchen. She showers afterward and douses her armpits with ample talcum powder before retreating to her room and turning on the television.

Oftentimes at the end of such stressful days, Shatu sits in front of the television and cries until she finally falls asleep. But now she only misses the vibrant noise of her house in Ghana, the dozens of people that lived in its compound, and the community feeling in the evenings—when residents gathered in the courtyard to snack on roasted peanuts while they exchanged tales and gossip until it was time to go to bed.

Even though Shatu's eyes are fixed on the TV set, her stare goes far beyond the tube's borders. American television, something Shatu was enamored of at first, no longer excites her; its sounds and flashy, fleeting images become a disturbing background noise that distracts rather than soothes her mind and heart. Yet, in her state of melancholy, Shatu is consoled by a goal she has only recently set her mind to achieve.

As she lies on her bed, apprehensive about Roger's impending call, Shatu vows to herself: I will not grow old in this country. I will not die here.

THE
MANHOOD TEST

On the day of Mr. Rafique's manhood test, he woke up at half past three in the morning, haunted by a dream of old women hawking phalluses of every size, shape, and color in the marketplace. He had barely slept, and remained lying on the hard-foamed couch in the sitting room, where he had slept for the past week. He pressed his limp penis gently—the way doctors press blood-pressure bulbs—hoping it would become fully erect, something he had not seen for three whole weeks.

Mr. Rafique became alert on hearing the loud crows of roosters in the courtyard, and was suddenly overpowered by the crippling fear that had tormented him since the day, about a week ago, when his wife had accused him of "unmanliness" at the chief's palace on Zongo Street. To verify the wife's allegations, the chief's *alkali*, or judge, had ordered Mr. Rafique to take the manhood test, a process that required Mr. Rafique to sleep with his wife before an appointed invigilator.

The test was scheduled for half past four that afternoon, and the mere thought of being naked with his wife and in the presence of a third person made Mr. Rafique's body numb. He brushed the fingers of his left hand around the edge of his penis. "Why are you treating me so?" he whispered to himself. "Eh, tell me! Why are you treating me so?" He lifted his head from the pillow to look at his crotch, as though he had expected the penis to answer. "What am I going to do, *yá Allah!*" he said, his voice now just above a whisper. "What am I going to do if I fail?"

Mr. Rafique lifted his arms and silently began to pray in the most distant region of his heart, where no one—not even the two angels said to be guarding each mortal day and night—could hear him. He prayed for a miracle to transform his limp phallus into a bouncing, fully erect one; he begged Allah to steer his destiny clear of the imminent humiliation that threatened to put him and his family to shame.

Mr. Rafique had been married for a little over eight months to a young but worldly woman named Zulaikha. Zulai, as she was called affectionately, was the last of four daughters of Baba Mina, a rich transportation business owner who used to live on Zongo Street. Like other once-very-poor-and-suddenly-turned-rich types, Baba Mina had moved to Nhyiaso, an expensive suburb of Kumasi, as soon as he became wealthy enough. He and his family visited their Zongo Street clan house only on weekends or whenever there was an important social function.

Zulaikha had been raised a spoiled child. Her parents—her mother especially—never denied her the things she desired. She wore expensive blouses and skirts instead of the traditional wrapper and *danchiki* worn by girls her age. And while some of her schoolmates drank water to quench both hunger and thirst during lunch break, Zulai ate boiled eggs and drank Fanta instead. At twelve, she had stood as the tallest girl among her age mates. She was slender, with a curvaceous figure that sent the eyes of men darting wherever she walked. Her thighs were muscular, supported by her long, athletic calves. Zulai also had deep, sensuous lips and eyes that were as clear as the moon at its brightest. Her cheeks were lean and dimpled, her eyebrows dark and silky. Her hair was always "permed," or straightened, its length touching her broad shoulders. By the time she was fourteen, Zulaikha's blouses could no longer contain her large breasts.

Her beauty, coupled with her family's riches, turned her into the most popular and desired teenager among the young men of Zongo Street. Before long, all the rich Muslim men in the city were knocking at her family's door, seeking the young girl's hand in marriage. Her father had planned to marry her off by the time she was sixteen, the usual marriage age for girls; but to her father's shock and disappointment, Zulai one by one rejected the dozen or so suitors he and his clan had chosen for her. She refused to see the men when they called, and she even went so far as to threaten to commit suicide if forced to marry a man she didn't choose herself. Her family then asked her to bring home her own suitor of choice, but she told them point blank that she was not ready to marry until she had finished middle school. Such a thing was unheard of from a young woman from Zongo Street.

As all of this unraveled, the street's young men were on a quest to see who would be the first to sleep with Zulaikha. And it wasn't long before one of them succeeded. His name was

Muntari, a twenty-one-year-old discogoer and school dropout who three years later found himself in the middle of a scandal when Zulaikha married his uncle, Mr. Rafique, who lived in the same compound with the young man.

Not long after her first sexual experience, Zulaikha quickly turned into a "sex monster," as some called her. Wild stories about her encounters with men abounded on the street. One was about how she slept with six men, who mounted her one after the other, but she was still left unsatisfied. Another story related how she had sex with a young man until he fainted and fell sick afterward. Soon Zulaikha's loose sexual behavior began to drag her clan's name in the mud. Her father then insisted she bring home a suitor, or he would marry her off to the man of his own choosing. By now the majority of the men who had earlier sought Zulaikha's hand had left off in their pursuit of her, afraid the girl's bad name might tarnish their reputations. A few of them persisted, though, and Mr. Rafique was one of them.

Most of the men who still sought Zulaikha's hand were rich ones also from Zongo Street, with two or three wives already, a practice sanctioned by Islam, the street's predominant religion. To Zulaikha, the idea of competing for a man's attention with two or three other women, along with its concomitant sexual starvation, seemed repugnant and stifling. So, even though Mr. Rafique was only a temporary clerk at a local sheanut butter cooperative union, he was the one she preferred. She was confident that her father would give him capital to start his own business, or at least offer him a position in his transport company. Zulai also had a genuine fascination with Mr. Rafique—and because of that, not even the knowledge of Mr. Rafique's illegitimate child, Najim, a seven-year-old boy who lived with his mother on Roman Hill, was enough to change her mind about him. Friends and a few family members tipped off Zulai that Najim's mother was a jilted lover who was still in love with Mr. Rafique and might cause her problems down the line in her marriage. But Zulai merely brushed the rumor aside. She was captivated by the fact that, unlike all the other suitors, Mr. Rafique was somewhat educated. He had attended school only up to Form Four (the equivalent of twelfth grade), but on a street like Zongo, where most of the folks never stepped foot in an English school classroom, Mr. Rafique and a few others were like one-eyed kings in the kingdom of the blind. But most important, Zulai was attracted to Mr. Rafique's handsome appearance. She liked the blazers and suits he wore, even on extremely hot days. In short, he conformed to her ideal of the handsome man: not too tall and not too short, either, and definitely without a pot belly, which she abhorred.

Not long after Zulai mentioned Mr. Rafique to her family, rumor reached their ears that he was a drunkard. The family didn't worry too much about this, hoping that "even if it is true, he will change his ways once he is married and saddled with the responsibility of looking after a family of his own," as Baba Mina said.

At the time of the wedding, Zulaikha was nineteen, three years older than the age at which most girls were married. She was only two years shy of finishing middle school, and some among Baba Mina's clan pleaded that he allow her to finish, but he said to them, "Of what use would schooling be to a woman? She is going to end up in the kitchen, after all!" With those words, Baba Mina sealed off the mouths of those who pleaded with him. Customary rituals were hastily carried out after that, paving the way for the marriage ceremony, which turned out to be one of the grandest functions the city of Kumasi had ever seen. Not that anyone expected less from the bride's wealthy father.

The marriage was on shaky ground from the very beginning, however. There were certain things Zulaikha had not given any thought to before, which suddenly developed into uncomfortable situations that were rife with the potential of creating serious problems for the marriage. The first involved having to live in the same compound as Muntari, the young man who had deflowered her. Although Muntari's room was located outside the main compound, he went inside at least twice each day to fetch hot bath water in the mornings and to pick up his supper in the evenings. And as much as Zulai attempted to ignore Muntari's presence in the compound, the two still ran into each other. Now a married woman, Zulai was quite embarrassed about this situation and lived with the constant fear of her premarital affair with Muntari being leaked out to her husband.

Zulai's other problem concerned something quite different. Like most buildings on Zongo Street, their house did not have a toilet, which meant that she had to be escorted about three hundred meters to the public latrine. For Zulaikha, who grew up using a glass toilet in the privacy of her parents' house, to empty one's bowels in the presence of five strangers, all squatting in a row, was not only barbaric and shameful, but depressing. She took care of that problem partly by going to the latrine only at night when the facility was often empty. She stuck to that

schedule, no matter how desperate she was with the need to re-
lieve herself during the day.

However, Zulai's third and last problem was more serious,
one that made the first two seem trivial. And here is what cre-
ated it:

Though Mr. Rafique's womanizing lifestyle prior to his mar-
riage had reached legendary status on Zongo Street, he had
somehow failed to keep his erection on the couple's first night
together. What occurred was peculiar and shocking to both hus-
band and wife, who had expected nothing short of fireworks on
their "maiden" encounter.

What exactly went wrong that night Mr. Rafique could not
understand. When his penis became limp in the middle of inter-
course, his first thought was to get up and send a child for a cup
of strong coffee from Mallam Sile's tea shop, hoping the hot bev-
erage would recharge his battery. But Zulaikha, who had heard
so much about Mr. Rafique's many affairs with women, was set
upon giving him a splendid first night. As he lay pondering, she
crawled all over him, caressing and kissing his chest and ribs. She
grabbed and rubbed Mr. Rafique's penis with her fingers, some-
thing he detested when his penis was not erect. He made some
gestures to thwart her moves, all the time thinking of the right
moment to get up and send for that revivifying cup of coffee. But
Zulaikha, who was as aroused as someone on a Malian aphro-
disiac, wouldn't let go of him. She became frustrated when she
realized her efforts weren't doing any good, and finally blamed it
all on herself, that she was too inexperienced for him. But Mr.
Rafique was busy entertaining fantasies of the women he had
slept with before, hoping he would be aroused by them. This

didn't work. Then, in a rather annoyed voice, he told Zulaikha: "Just lie down and stop moving your hands on me like a snake, you hear?" After that the couple lay awake in awkward silence for the rest of the night. They stared at the ceiling and listened to the sounds of their breathing until the rooster's first crow at dawn.

Strangely enough, the next morning, Mr. Rafique's penis became as erect as a lamppost on his way to the bath house. It remained hard for the rest of the day while he was at work. In fact he had to use several creative methods in order to hide the bulge in his trousers. That relieved and reassured him that his inability the night before was caused by anxiety, which he thought he could overcome easily. I just have to dominate her completely, he said to himself.

On the second night, Mr. Rafique jumped into their bed with a full erection. He was all ready to redeem himself, and to prove to Zulai that he was not an *adaakwa*, a pansy. I'll show her that I am the man of the two of us, he thought as he pulled the bedside string to switch off the light. He cautioned himself not to let "her have any control, the way I foolishly allowed her to last night." But no sooner had Mr. Rafique entered his wife he lost his stiffness again. Suddenly his manhood began to shrink like a popped balloon. Zulai used every trick she knew, but her efforts were futile. Soon, Mr. Rafique's penis became the shadow of a penis, a mere token of his manhood. The same thing happened on the next night and the one that followed.

After the fourth night's fiasco, Mr. Rafique drank some Alafia bitters, and Zulaikha too acquired some herbal scents and erotic lavenders, which she hoped would boost their lust and desire for each other; but that, too, didn't do them any good. What was most upsetting to Mr. Rafique was the fact that, as soon as he prepared to leave home for work in the morning, his penis became erect. He tried to keep his anger and frustration to himself, not quite sure how to share a story like this with anyone. He therefore decided that the only thing that would help him was prayer. And so he prayed.

A month and a half later, the couple's situation remained the same. Mr. Rafique contemplated turning to other women—old girlfriends or the fancy, expensive prostitutes at Hotel de Kingsway, one of the finest in all of Ghana, which he frequented before his marriage—to at least clarify whether his inability occurred only with Zulaikha. But he couldn't bring himself to betray his wife, with whom he was already falling in love, despite their problems.

Eventually Mr. Rafique consoled himself that "Allah is the cause of all things," and that "He alone knows why this is happening." He thought he was either being punished for the promiscuous life he had led during his bachelor days or that Allah was just testing him and waiting for the right time to bless and bring happiness to his marriage, as His Prophet Muhammad promises in the *Hadiths*—the *Book of Traditions*.

Though Mr. Rafique and his wife were greatly saddened by this turn of events, they recoiled from making it known or seeking help—he because of his male pride and Zulaikha out of fear that more fingers would be pointed at her if news of their problem became known. And so, the couple continued to live in their erotic disenchantment for the next two months, during which a severe tension began to grow between the two. They fought and bickered regularly, often over the most trivial things. For his part, Mr. Rafique had—not without profound sadness—already given up hope that he would be able to lie with his wife. He spent most of his time away from the house, either at work during the day or in front of Rex Cinema in the evening, where he played *da-me*, a complicated version of checkers, with friends until well after midnight. Mr. Rafique's sorrows grew even worse: Zulai acquired the habit of waiting for his arrival each night so she could pick fights with him—fights in which she did nothing but assail his inability.

As time went by, Mr. Rafique assumed the un-Islamic and ungodly act of blaming the "old witches" on the street for his problems. He thought of having a talk with his wife, to tell her "face-to-face" that her aggressive sex manner was the main cause of his inability. But in the end he feared coming across as a wimp with such an open admission of unmanliness. So he remained silent.

Night after night Mr. Rafique lay awake on his bed next to his wife, staring into the darkness and contemplating the doom that awaited him the moment Zulaikha opened her mouth to her folks about his inability. He knew that was bound to happen sooner or later, unless a dramatic change occurred, which he couldn't fathom.

One Thursday morning, after three months of bridal incarceration—the period when young brides were prohibited from leaving the house without an escort, usually a girl or a woman from the man's family—Zulaikha's veil-lifting ceremony took place. It marked the partial lifting of the ban on her movement, as she was limited to visiting her parents, attending naming ceremonies or funerals, and most important, walking to the public latrine without her usual escorts of young girls. In another three months, Zulaikha would be permitted to go wherever she wished to go, since she was naturally expected to be carrying Mr. Rafique's child by then. This custom—traditional rather than religious, which demanded that brides be virgins—enforced a young bride's loyalty to her husband during the first six months of marriage.

Soon after the veil-lifting ceremony Mr. Rafique and Zulaikha took to quarreling more often, cursing one another in front of people in the compound. Zulai considered revealing Mr. Rafique's problem to someone in her clan, but decided against it, afraid that it might be taken as a ploy for divorce, as used by some women. But she knew she must do something, not only about her husband's inability, but also about her involuntary celibacy. She began to have fantasies of Muntari, and even thought of seducing him into her bed. The young man obviously didn't want to get caught in the middle of a marriage scandal; as if he had gotten wind of Zulaikha's designs, he departed for Agégé, joining the exodus that swept away Ghana's young men and women to the Nigerian city, in search of a better life. But the couple's problems grew even bigger.

One evening, Mr. Rafique said good-bye to his wife and left the house for the cinema-front to play *da-me* with friends. He realized on reaching the game place that he had left behind his pack of cigarettes. He immediately returned home. But when Mr. Rafique arrived Zulaikha was not in the house. Zulai, who had gone to the latrine and didn't expect her husband back until much later, had stayed talking to friends she had met on her way home. Mr. Rafique picked up the pack but decided to wait for his wife's return—he had been suspicious of her comings and goings lately. He paced around the living room, his mind brimming with anger. He glanced at the wall clock at two-minute intervals, growing angrier each time.

Half an hour passed and Zulaikha had not returned. The longer Mr. Rafique waited, the more distrustful and suspicious he became. He stormed out of the room in a great fury and walked across the courtyard to the compound's main entrance. He stood there like a sentry, and lighted one cigarette after another while he cursed the housefolks, including his mother, Hindu, who had not been able to leave her room for nine years, crippled by a mysterious disease. Mr. Rafique shouted obscenities at the top of his voice, calling the housefolks "hypocrites and traitors."

"If it isn't hypocrisy what is it then, when your own people can't even keep an eye on your woman, eh? Tell me!" he yelled, looking at the children who surrounded him, as if he expected them to console him. "All of them, they are backbiters; I know they are waiting to see my downfall. But she will see when she returns tonight! I'll show her the thing that prevents women from growing beards!" He was screaming and waving his fists at no one in particular.

The housefolks knew better than to say a word to Mr. Rafique. When he was angry he stopped speaking Hausa altogether and shouted at them in English—of which nobody understood even a word—and threatened to bring in his military friends to "discipline everyone." Though Mr. Rafique had never acted on his boast, people were still scared, because the military friends, whose sight alone could send one panicking, visited him dressed in full combat gear, with guns hanging from their shoulders and dynamite dangling from their waistbands. The housefolks didn't say a word when Mr. Rafique ranted and raved about his wife's absence. They merely sat and watched from their verandahs.

About an hour after Mr. Rafique returned home, Zulaikha came trotting into the compound. Mr. Rafique immediately pounced on her, seizing her dress and demanding to know where she had been.

"Let go of me, O! What is all this for?" she said. "Making a fool out of yourself again, eh?"

"Who are you talking to like that, you bastard woman! Where've you been? I say, tell me where you have been all this time!"

"Where do you think I went to other than the backhouse?" she replied, and gently slapped his hands to free her dress from his grip.

"Look, don't vex me more than you have already!" he shouted, the veins sticking out of his neck. "Was it only the latrine that took you more than one hour? I say, tell me where you have been, before I take action on you!"

"What action are you capable of taking—look at him! I beg, don't scream at me like that! Am I not allowed to talk to my friends on the road when I meet—" He didn't let her finish.

"You liar! You pathetic liar! A horrible liar you are! Daughter of liars!" he screamed, waving his index finger in her face.

Much later that night, before the elders, Zulaikha claimed that it was by mistake, but whether her claim was true or not, she slapped Mr. Rafique's hand as he waved it in her face. He in turn hit her in the face. But hardly had his hand dropped before she, too, responded with a blow that was three times stronger than his. Mr. Rafique staggered and fell to the ground. The housefolks screamed in shock. What would have ensued would have been disastrous, but one of Mr. Rafique's military friends lived in the next compound; and it was he who overheard the fight and walked over and separated the two. But the couple resumed fighting as soon as they returned to their living room. That night they kept the entire household awake, throwing their furniture around and screaming at each other. They fought until two o'clock in the morning, when the chief's *wazeer*, or right-hand man, came and separated them. Zulaikha spent what little remained of the night with her in-law, Mr. Rafique's lame mother, while he remained in his room and ranted until the *asubá* worship.

Early the next day, the chief's *alkali* ordered Zulaikha to return to her family for a three-day *yáji*, or mediation period. One might have expected Zulai to reveal her husband's inability to her family during the *yáji*, but she did not. However, her folks quickly noticed her flat belly, and without asking her a single question, concluded that her barrenness was the reason Zulai and her husband fought so frequently. The family immediately visited a spiritual *mallam*, or medicine man, who proclaimed that Zulai was visited by *men of night*, bad spirits who copulated with married women in their sleep and destroyed their pregnancies.

While Zulaikha was with her family, Mr. Rafique mustered enough courage to see a *mallam* for his problem. The medicine man told Mr. Rafique that his inability was a curse, one thrown at him by a rival who had wanted to marry Zulaikha. The *mallam* never informed him who the mysterious rival was, but he gave Mr. Rafique a talisman and asked him to place it under his mattress before sleeping with his wife the next time. "*Wallahi*, this is the end of your problem, my son . . . no more sleepy-sleepy manhood," the medicine man swore, and gazed at the ceiling in supplication to Allah, as he handed Mr. Rafique the tiny red amulet.

On the night Zulaikha returned, Mr. Rafique was confident that the *mallam's* proclamation would manifest itself. But Mr. Rafique once again lost his erection while in action. This particular failure became the straw that broke the "camel's hunched back," as Hamda-Wán, Zongo Street's infamous latrine cleaner, would say when things went awry. The next morning, Mr. Rafique felt he had been conned by the *mallam* and the spiritual bodies he had invoked for his "miracles." What was worse, Mr. Rafique felt slighted by Allah, to whom he prayed daily to save his marriage. At this point he gave up all hope and waited for the day when Allah, in His infinite mercy, would make good His promise to help those who cry out to Him in their times of need.

As time went by, Zulai came to accept that nothing could be done to improve her husband's inability. And after a bitter inner struggle, she decided the only thing that would prevent her name from being dragged into the mud was to disclose his problems to the elders. The sooner I do this, the better for me, she thought one night. I must let his people and the streetfolks know that I am not the 'bottomless pit' they think I am. . . . My belly can carry a seed, but only if he plants it!"

The following day she went to the chief's palace and lodged a formal complaint with the *alkali*, charging her husband with "unmanliness." According to Islamic *shari'a* law, a wife can seek divorce from her husband on three conditions: (1) if he doesn't provide *chi da sha*, or food and drink, for her, (2) if she deems there is no love between herself and her husband, and (3) if he is *sick*, or impotent. A husband, on the other hand, is not bound by any strict stipulation and may divorce his wife at will.

Zulai's complaint quickly became news on Zongo Street. Not many believed the wife's accusations, as Najim was clear testimony to Mr. Rafique's manliness. At a hearing in the palace of the Muslim chief on Zongo Street, Mr. Rafique insisted that his manhood was in perfect condition and that his wife's accusation was false, "a mere excuse . . . so that the conniving wench can seek a divorce from me," he said. Zulaikha challenged her husband: "He is not a man, and he knows this himself! Believe me! By Allah, he is not a man!" she swore. The couple began to fight in front of the most revered elders; they screamed and raised fingers in one another's faces. The fight was separated, but by the end of the hearing it became impossible even for the wise jurors to decide who was telling the truth. So the *alkali* decided to give the couple six weeks to either solve their problem or report back to him if they failed to do so.

· · ·

The weeks that followed were quite brutal for Mr. Rafique. He tried to seal his ears to the countless rumors being spread about him and his marriage. At home, the fights between him and Zulai became regular entertainment for the housefolks, who sat and laughed watching the tragicomedy unfold. Then, after an ugly fight that lasted all night, Zulaikha resolved that she would be better off without a husband. The next morning she paid her second visit to the *alkali* and demanded a divorce from Mr. Rafique on the grounds that he still wasn't a man.

Now, on Zongo Street, divorces of that kind were granted only after the accused husband was proven "unmanly" by a neutral person, usually an old woman appointed by the *alkali*. The *lafiree*, the name given to the old woman, sat in the same room and observed closely as the husband made love to his wife. She would later report her observations to the *alkali*, who made the final decision in such cases.

Mr. Rafique's test date was scheduled a week from the day of Zulaikha's divorce petition. It was on a Wednesday, a day generally perceived as ill-omened by the streetfolks—though no one knew exactly why. And since "days never fail to make their weekly appearance," the test date approached rather too fast for Mr. Rafique, though it seemed to have arrived too slowly for the streetfolks, who were more eager than ever to just see *something* happen to *someone*. Long before it was four-thirty on the appointed day, the palace front was filled with news and rumor-mongers, who seemed just as apprehensive as the poor husband

and wife who now found themselves in a public drama from which they could not escape being a part of.

About an hour after he woke up on the morning of the test Mr. Rafique was still lying on the couch, his half-erect penis cupped in his left hand. His eyes were dry and itchy from lack of sleep; his mind fatigued by the phalluses he had seen in his nightmares; his body tired from a week of sleeping on the couch. He heard the muezzin's incantations, "*Allahu Akbar, Allahu Akbar*" — God is great! God is great!—calling the faithful to *asuba* worship, the first of their five daily supplications to the Creator. He gently rubbed his penis as he listened: "*Assalát hairi minal-naum! Assalát hairi minal-naum!*" —Worship is better than sleep! Worship is better than sleep!

The mellifluous, melancholy, yet commanding voice of the crier soothed Mr. Rafique's heart momentarily, ridding him of the thoughts of the impending test. But this didn't last too long, his mind gradually drifting back to his manhood fixation. He sat upright and began to pray: "Let my enemies be disappointed and ashamed of their enmity today, *yá Allah!*" He lifted his arms in the air, with a face full of self-pity. "And to those who doubt my 'manliness,' *yá Allah,*" he continued, "prove to them that all power comes from you. Equip me with the strength to perform this test, to which I am maliciously being subjected!"

He closed the prayer by reciting *Áyatul-Kursiyyu,* a verse deemed by most clerics as the second most powerful in the Koran, one that is supposed to work wonders in solving all kinds of problems. Finally, Mr. Rafique raised his arms in the air, spat on his open palms, and rubbed them gently on his face. He murmured, "Ámin," lay back on the couch, and resumed caressing his penis. Before long, Mr. Rafique was once again lost in his activity. But the muezzin's voice, distant and echoing, again reminded Mr. Rafique that it was almost time for worship.

Ash-hadu al-láiláha illallá! I bear witness there is no God besides Allah!

As if spurred on by the muezzin's cries, Mr. Rafique's penis suddenly began to harden. A minute later, it was as erect and solid as an unripe green plantain—crooked and curved toward his right thigh. Never before in his thirty eight years had his penis been this hard; it was bewildering. He moved his butt sideways and spread his legs apart, so as to make room for his bulging crotch. Filled with an inner joy, he was almost driven by a sudden desire to walk into the bedroom and thrust his way into his wife. But a second thought advised him against it. He decided to wait until the test, "before the eyes of that old *lafiree* and the entire street. Then I will prove to my wife and all my enemies that I am a full-grown man."

It then dawned on Mr. Rafique that the morning worship was about to begin. In one movement he sprang from the couch and got into his prayer robe, which concealed the bulge in his loose slacks. He slipped his feet into rubber slippers and sprinted out of the room and into the breezy, dew-scented dawn. Outside, a handful of lazy-boned roosters—that had just awakened—crowed. Mr. Rafique ran all the way to the mosque, reciting *dhikr* under his breath.

. . .

Zulaikha was already at the chief's palace when Mr. Rafique arrived at four. She was accompanied by two middle-aged women from her clan, and they sat in the large, high-ceilinged lounge of the palace and waited for Zulai, who was being briefed by the *alkali* at the time of Mr. Rafique's arrival. Mr. Rafique ignored them. "Hypocrites," he whispered, stealing a mean glance at them. "That's what they are, all of them! They act as if they like you, when all they are after is your downfall!" He found an unoccupied bench in the corner and sat to wait for his turn to be briefed by the chief's judge.

The meeting with the *alkali* lasted no more than five minutes, and as Mr. Rafique walked through the foyer to the test room, he saw at least three dozen faces staring at him through the lounge's many windows. He felt as if the entire city of Kumasi was watching him, eagerly awaiting his downfall. Ever so determined to redeem himself "in the eyes of my enemies," and to "put them all to shame, by Allah," Mr. Rafique ignored the stares and walked confidently into the long, wide corridor that led into the palace's courtyard. He began to think that the presence of the *lafiree* would actually be to his advantage, because Zulaikha—who would not want to be perceived as a whore by the old woman—would lie still as she received him, in the exact manner expected of a married woman. The test suddenly appeared exciting to Mr. Rafique, who felt blood surging through his half-erect penis as he walked closer to the test room.

After leaving the *alkali's* office, the old lady and Zulaikha walked directly to the test room, located at the northern end of the palace compounds. The palace building was composed of three large rectangular houses, each with its own compound and courtyard and rooms numbering up to twenty-four. The test room had only one window, which faced the almost-vacant courtyard. The interior of the room was brightly lit by a three-foot fluorescent tube. A double-sized kapok bed was tucked in the left corner of the room and a small table sat beside the bed. The invigilator's chair was placed facing the bed, and in a way that the *lafiree* would be able to have a clear glimpse of what went on.

Mr. Rafique paused on reaching the door. "*Assalaamu-alaikum!*" he said and waited for a response. The door was opened by the old woman, who peeked outside. Despite the freckles all over her wrinkled face, the *lafiree* looked healthy for her age. She was sixty-eight. Her gracious smile, which exposed two gaps in her front teeth, seemed fake to Mr. Rafique, who simply saw her as another of his enemies. Responding to her warm, inviting smile, he grinned maliciously.

"Come inside," the *lafiree* said, though she was quite aware of Mr. Rafique's animosity. "Call me when you are ready to begin. I will be waiting outside." She smiled as she walked past him.

Mr. Rafique went into the test room.

Meanwhile, a large crowd had gathered outside the chief's palace to be part of this historical event—for such cases were brought only once in a blue moon to the chief. The older folks on the street claimed that of the few cases that had been brought before to the chief's court, Mr. Rafique's was the only one wherein the couple had actually decided to perform the test. In earlier cases, many husbands were said to have given their wives a divorce instead of having sex with them in front of a stranger.

A number of women—peanut, yam, and ginger-beer

vendors—congregated near the palace gates, and a garrulous woman who claimed to be the best friend of Zulaikha's mother captured their full attention with her story: "The girl's mother did confide in me that the spiritualist they visited told them that the man's *thing* was long ago cooked and eaten by witches, at one of their weekly feasts," the woman told her rapt audience. "And would you believe it if I told you that it was no one but his mother who took the *thing* to the feast? Which goes to show that she herself is a witch." The woman lowered her voice. "No wonder she has been lying in a grass bed for nine years! But you didn't hear this from me, O! Okay?" But the rumormonger then went on to describe to the vendors (in full, graphic details) how Mr. Rafique's penis was cut, prepared, and eaten by the witches. The garrulous woman's listeners gasped at every sentence and wondered how she came about this information. But none of them questioned her, afraid they might upset her.

Gathered near the vendors was a group of young men from about the ages of sixteen to twenty-three. They, too, speculated about the test. One of them swore that he saw Mr. Rafique as he walked into the palace, and that "his prick looked as if it would tear itself right through his trousers. I tell you, man, that was how hard he was!" Then he challenged his listeners to a bet of a hundred cedis each if they doubted his word that Mr. Rafique would pass the test. None of his listeners showed interest in betting, though they all rooted for Mr. Rafique, just as most of the women and girls on the street rooted for Zulaikha.

· · ·

Zulai's eyes met her husband's as he entered the room. She had not seen him since that morning, when he left for work. She lowered her head and shifted uneasily toward the end of the bed. Mr. Rafique just stood there, not saying a word. Zulai lifted her face, and their eyes met again. He shrugged his shoulders and moved his eyebrows up and down, gesturing—or rather signaling—for them to begin what they had come to do. Zulaikha felt like a whore—a very cheap one, for that matter, given that the entire city of Kumasi knew what was about to happen between her and her husband; and the fact that there were people outside the palace waiting for the results made her feel even cheaper. Hatred surged through her, not for Mr. Rafique, but for the streetfolks.

Then things took a rather unexpected turn. Zulai bowed her head and suddenly felt a tenderness toward her husband and even blamed herself for all of their marital misfortune. *Our marriage has brought nothing but ruin to him; the disgrace that awaits him once the test is over! I wish I knew what to do to make him do well,* she said to herself. *Maybe I should tell the old woman that I was lying about his manhood.* But she also knew it was too late for her to alter what everyone on the street already knew—the horses were already lined up before the open field, and the derby could not be canceled.

For Mr. Rafique's part, looking at his estranged wife suddenly turned him soft, not between his legs, as one might have expected, but in his chest—in his heart. *Why the hurt and the vendetta? Why not forgive everyone, so that you can move on with your life?* Mr. Rafique couldn't believe the thoughts he was having, and was perplexed as well as relieved by these questions.

Zulai wondered what was going on. She lifted her head to steal a glance at her husband, whose eyes were directed at her. The two were face-to-face, eyes locked. And Mr. Rafique saw in his wife's face all the qualities that had drawn him to her some eight months ago: her confidence, charm, and warm personality. As he looked at her large, seductive eyes, he felt an intense passion for her—it was a joyous, yet aching, sensation, since he still couldn't rid his mind of the pain of the past months. Mr. Rafique saw himself at an emotional crossroad, not knowing whether to "perform the test or to renounce everything—the test, sex in general, Zulai, the people of Zongo Street, and anything that had been in the way of my happiness." Mr. Rafique resolved to renounce it all, and prepared himself to break the news to his wife and the old woman; he would grant Zulai the divorce she sought.

By separating myself from the spell sex and love cast on people, I can continue to love her, spiritually, wholly, for the rest of our lives, thought Mr. Rafique. He was just about to speak to Zulai when he heard the *lafiree*'s voice: "Are you two ready?"

"Yes," Mr. Rafique answered calmly.

Zulaikha, utterly confused as to what would happen next, looked away from the door. The *lafiree*—who had expected to see a lot more than what she saw—seemed disappointed.

"I have changed my mind," Mr. Rafique said, avoiding Zulaikha's eyes.

"What are you talking about?" the old woman cried, grabbing his forearm.

"I don't really know, to tell you the truth, but I won't do it even if you leave the room." He paused, glanced at his wife, and continued. "And I hereby grant her the divorce, one, two, three times!"

"Wait, Rafiku," the old woman said. "Why do you want to do this to yourself? You know what the Zongo people will say, don't you?"

"Yes, I do! But, for all I care, they can say whatever they want to say! My heart tells me I am doing a good thing. That's what matters to me, not what the Zongolese think." The *lafiree* shuddered at Mr. Rafique's pronouncement. And Zulaikha, who one might have expected to rejoice, sat with eyes half-closed and brows tightly knit. Mr. Rafique took a step toward Zulaikha. He lowered his head, and with his left palm on his chest extended his right arm to her. "*Ma-assalám,*" he said politely before turning to walk out of the room. The women stared at each other and then at his back, still unable to make head or tail of what had taken place.

No sooner had Mr. Rafique walked through the palace gates than rumor started floating around that he had failed the manhood test. By the next day, there were half a dozen new stories, each one a slight variation, salted and spiced as it went from one mouth to another. Some rumors claimed that Mr. Rafique had actually passed the test, but had soon afterward pronounced the divorce, as a means of revenge on his wife. One swore that Mr. Rafique's "pen had run out of ink" in the middle of the test. Another maintained that he had failed miserably, that he "wasn't even able to get his *thing* up," to begin with, and that he had never been a *man*, and that Najim was someone else's son after all, a child forced on him by "his harlot-mother" because the real culprit had denied responsibility for the pregnancy.

The *lafiree*, who had apparently noticed the bulge in Mr. Rafique's trousers when he entered the test room, defended him. She swore by her many years and the *strength* of her dead husband that "the young man Rafiku is a real man! I saw his trouser-front with my two eyes, and believe me, I can tell a real *man* when I see one!"

So much for the old woman's attempt to tell the truth of what she saw. The street's rascals nicknamed her "Madam-real-manhood." And to the chagrin of the poor lady, that nickname followed her to her grave.

Life went on as usual on Zongo Street after the dust of this drama settled. Ironically, Zulaikha's life didn't change much afterward. A rumor soon circulated that she was the one who indeed "killed" Mr. Rafique's penis, seeing as he was virile enough to father a child before he met her. But Zulai wasn't bothered by these assertions, and continued to live her life in the foolhardy manner she had once lived. She threw away the headscarf worn by married Muslim women and divorcées, exposing her permed hair to the world, and refused to be classified as a "*bazawara*," a term that had taken on a derogatory meaning to describe a divorced woman—often seen as either one carrying emotional baggage or as damaged goods that men should try to avoid at any cost. She didn't marry again until six years later, when she was twenty-five, and it was to a rich man in the capital city, Accra, over two hundred miles away.

Mr. Rahque's life went on, too, though in a rather different manner. After he left the palace he had headed straight to Apala Goma, the beer parlor down on Bompata Road. He felt as relieved as a donkey that has returned from a long journey and finally has the load it carried taken off its back. Mr. Rafique felt even more relieved and freer than the donkey, because the animal never has the choice of carrying or not carrying a load in the first place. If it does, it will not carry the load at all. Who likes to suffer? But an ass is an ass, always at the mercy of its master, whereas I am my own master! As Mr. Rafique contemplated in this manner, he stepped into the doorway of the drinking parlor. Henceforth, I am going to live my life the way I see fit, he thought while he waited for a double shot of straight gin, the first of many drinks that night. By the time Mr. Rafique left the bar, around a quarter past midnight, he was quite drunk. Fortunately for him, the rascals who had the habit of thrashing drunks at night had vacated the street. It surprised Mr. Rafique that as drunk as he was, his thoughts were still clear. He vividly recalled the incidents of the whole day, and grinned to himself.

Upon reaching his house, Mr. Rafique found the main gate locked from the inside. To avoid trouble between him and Mamman Salisu—Mr. Rafique's self-righteous half brother who denounced his drinking with religious vehemence—Mr. Rafique proceeded farther down the compound, to the small concretized prayer lot where the boys and young men in the neighborhood slept on very hot nights. There was a common saying among the streetfolks: "Men who want to command respect should not sleep in the company of children." Mr. Rafique laughed and walked to the back of the lot, where straw mats were kept in an old oil drum. He selected a mat and spread it in an empty space between two young men who were both his nephews. After removing his shoes, he curled up on his right side. He closed his eyes and placed his hands between his legs. Mr. Rafique had never before experienced such inner peace. They will not get me again! They can drown themselves if they don't like the way I live! he said to himself at that moment when consciousness crosses the path of sleep in their tireless effort to bring calm to the pulsing heart of Man.

THE
TRUE ARYAN

When I stepped out of the Liquid Lounge Club around three in the morning, only a few stragglers were out on the street—homeless people pushing their overflowing carts, musicians and bartenders heading home after a grueling night in some crowded, smoke-filled joint, and drugged-out clubgoers looking for the few places left open to buy food or something more to drink. I didn't expect to have a problem finding a cab at such a late hour, which wasn't the case during the morning and evening rush—or around midnight on Fridays and Saturdays—when the city's cabbies almost never stopped for a black fare.

Two cabs were parked right in front of the club. I lugged my two *djimbe* drums, talking drum, and percussion instrument bag toward the cab in front. The driver of the first cab, who chatted excitedly with the driver of a second cab, waved at me. "Come here, my frien'," he said, his voice thick with an Eastern Mediterranean accent—Greece, Albania, or even Turkey. Who knows? He was burly and looked to be in his early fifties.

My behavior over the years toward the cabbies who actually

picked me up could best be described as passive-aggressive, and sometimes downright hostile. The cabbies only picked me up because the streets were empty and business was slow; I didn't feel compelled to be nice to any one of them. So, even though this cabbie seemed friendly enough, I still found it difficult to abandon my usual disposition.

As I made my way to the trunk of the cab, the cabbie offered to help. "I take care of this, you take the small bag inside," he said, and took away my *djimbe* drums and dumped them in the car's trunk.

"Goin' to Borooklyn?" he asked.

"Yes, Park Slope," I answered, proceeding to the rear passenger door.

The car smelled of a freshly sprayed air freshener, though the remnant of the cigarette odor it was meant to camouflage still lurked in its interior. My eyes were already itchy and watery from the smoke that permeated the poorly ventilated basement of the club, where I played a weekly gig with Fatima, my Afro-Jazz quintet. While I waited for the driver, I started to think about my day job. I had to be in at ten o'clock. The thought of having to go to work, and of staring at a computer monitor for hours designing and updating corporate Web sites, increased my fatigue.

"What is yo'r address?" the cabbie asked when he got into the car.

I answered curtly, hoping to send across the message that I wasn't particularly in the mood for a hot political debate—for which New York cabbies were famous. He didn't get my meaning.

"Wher' ar' you from," he asked.

"Brooklyn," I answered.

"No-no-no, I mean wher' did you come from?"

"Oh, I am from Ghana, in West—"

"I know Ghana," he interrupted. "I have many, many taxi-driver friends from Ghana."

"I see."

"I am from Armenia," he continued, his face beaming with a proud smile.

"I see," I said again.

We were now at a traffic light. I looked out the window, hoping to discourage the cabbie from asking me any further questions.

"So you ar' a misician, huh?" he asked.

I drew in a deep breath, sighed, then answered, "Yes."

"Hey, you don't wanna talk to me, my frien'? Me, I love people."

Who cares, I thought, but then turned and said, "No, I am just tired . . ."

"Listen," said the driver. He turned and looked at me through the car's glass partition. "Come and sit in the front. Come, my friend."

"No, that's okay," I said. But as soon as we turned left on Ninth Street, the cabbie slammed on the brakes and double-parked next to a Volkswagen sedan. The handful of cars behind us hooted relentlessly.

"Fuck them," he said laughingly, and to me, coolly, "Come to the front, my frien'."

I opened the door and stepped out. After I had settled in the front seat and shut the passenger door, he said, "This is much better, my frien'. You see, me, I like all the people in the world. Doesn't matter wher' you come from." He looked at me, as if to gauge my reaction to his statement.

I maintained a blank expression.

"I know, I know," he continued, as if conceding defeat in an argument, "that many of us don't pick up black people, but me, I pick up any person that stops me."

I thought he might be playing the role of the guilty white ethnic type that has real sympathy for blacks. Maybe he was genuine in his sympathy, and just as I sometimes behaved "properly" to make up for the bad image of blacks, he, too, was putting on a p.c. face to make up for the behavior of the bad eggs in his profession. But I didn't give a damn! Just leave me alone! I thought. Though when I opened my mouth to speak, I only said, "That's awfully nice of you."

"Yes, me am very nice," he said, smiling. "You can smoke her', you know," he added and suddenly produced a pack of a foreign-looking brand of cigarettes from his shirt's pocket.

"No, thanks, I don't smoke."

"You can smoke anything you want. I have some pot, too. No?"

"No, thanks, I don't smoke that, either."

"What is 'rong with you, a misician who does not smoke anything at all?" He laughed hoarsely.

He lifted a cigarette to his lips and as he searched for the lighter, asked, "Do you mind?"

"No," I answered.

As he lit the fag at the next traffic light, I quickly dialed my home number. The answering machine came on after three rings. "Shit," I said under my breath before leaving a message for Frances, my live-in girlfriend.

"Hey, it's me. Just calling to let you know I'm on my way home. I hope I didn't wake you up. See you soon."

Although Frances assured me the tobacco and sweaty smells that trailed me after such late-night gigs didn't bother her, and had implored me to jump into bed beside her when I returned, I often felt guilty waking her up in the middle of the night when I came home from a gig. But tonight, more than any other I could remember in a while, I needed Frances's touch and loving care.

I put the phone in my pocket and decided to tune out the Armenian, diverting my attention to pressing issues in my life. Two months ago my parents had called with the news that they had picked "a good-natured girl from a very good family" back home in Ghana for me to marry. We argued, and I hadn't called them for the past month. And as depressed and upset as I was, I still hadn't been able to tell Frances what my parents were thinking. We had lived together for three years.

But the Armenian was not one to be tuned out so easily.

"You see, we artist ar' di'ferent, we don't hate," he said as soon as he realized I had finished with my phone call.

I nodded, and at the same time cursed under my breath for not placing another call immediately.

"I am misician, too, you know," he continued.

"I see," I said.

"You know zurna?"

"Zurna? No idea. Is it a style of music you—"

"No-no-no-no, it is ins'rument. Zurna is the firs' soprano saxophone ever made, from my people," he said, rolling the R's in his words with emphasis.

"So, that is the instrument you play? The zurna?"

"No, my frien'," he said. "You're not saying it right. We call it *zurr-nah!*"

"*Zur-na*," I repeated.

"No-no-no-no, my frien', *zurr-nah*."

"Okay, *zurr-nah!*" I said stressing the R's as long as I could and punctuating the "ah" in the same manner he did.

"That's right, my frien'," he screamed excitedly.

"Whatever," I muttered. "So, is *zurr-nah* the instrument you play?" I asked.

"I play ever'thing: zurna, duduk, davul, dhol, sulich; you bring it, I play it," he said, gesticulating wildly with his right hand. "I even play the kanoon. You know the kanoon, right?"

"No, I don't know the kanoon."

"You ar' misician and you don' know the kanoon?" he asked. "You see, they hide many things about the history of my people. Kanoon is the firs' harpsichord, and it is also created by my people."

I wondered what next this zealous guy would tell me his people created. Nevertheless, I nodded my head in approval of all the wonderful achievements of the cabbie's great Armenian people—first soprano sax, first harpsichord, and by default, the original inventors of the piano. But wait a minute, I thought. That's not all true. The balafon was the first harpsichord.

"But, excuse me," I said to the cabbie. "Have you heard of the kora?"

"*Kora?* Music insrument?" he asked.

"Yes, it is a harp-lute with up to twenty-five strings, and with a big gourd base. It is from West Africa."

"But what about it?" he asked.

"Well, my version of history has it that the kora was the most original harpischord, and therefore the first piano."

"No-no-no-no, no civilization beats Armenia," he screamed. "Ever'body knows we made the firs' harpsichord, the firs' piano ever!"

"Well, we can agree to disagree on that," I said.

We were now at the final traffic light before the Manhattan Bridge, at the intersection of the Bowery and Canal Street in Chinatown. I could tell the cabbie was more than a little ticked off by our disagreement. He smoked his cigarette quietly, his face sullen, apparently thinking about what to say next.

When the light turned green, he sped onto the bridge ramp so fast that we almost hit two garbage trucks that drove along-side us. He screamed, "Fuck you," at the driver and kept going. He drove erratically for a while and almost got into an accident by cutting too closely in front of another speeding cab. And throughout all of this he didn't say a word to me, a gesture I truly welcomed. Our disagreement, it seemed, had done the unin-tended trick for me; he was finally leaving me alone.

I turned my face toward the window to soak in the beauty of the Lower Manhattan skyline. It was a dark and humid night, and the lights of the World Trade Center buildings resembled shooting stars. Somehow, looking at the city's skyline always filled me with a sense of success and self-importance—the hope that my music would give rise to the American dream I strived for.

Then at mid-bridge the cabbie blurted, "You know Armenia?"

Here we go again, I thought, and paused briefly before I asked him, "What do you mean?"

"You know anything about Armenia?"

"Of course," I intoned. "Wasn't it part of the former USSR, next to Georgia?"

"You know the map verry, verry well," he said.

I gave him a fake smile, wondering about his intentions.

My head ached and my eyes burned from the cigarette ashes and smoke the cabbie blew in my face each time he moved his arms or exhaled.

"But, yes, yes, I am glad you said *former* Soviet Union. No mor', ever again!" He paused and flipped the cigarette butt out the open window. "Many, many people try to dominate us for centuries, but we ar' strong people. We ar' the original people of the whole Asia and the Middle East," he continued, his voice more animated. "You see, the, the founder of Turkey—"

"Ataturk?" I said, quoting from Orhan Pamuk's *The Black Book*, which I had, by a mere coincidence, just finished reading a few days before.

"You know too much, my friend. You are a verry, verry smart black, err, err," he stopped himself in midsentence, then added, "misician." The Armenian seemed to have suddenly realized the folly in calling me a smart black man. Not knowing how to proceed, he could only laugh uncomfortably. A few empty moments passed between us.

"You'r' right, but, let me correct you. Ataturk is the founder of, err, modern Turkey. Befor' Ataturk, before Turkey itself, ther' was us, the Armenians. And Hamid was the, was the, original Sultan." He stammered on.

Despite my obvious lack of interest in his ever-expanding story, the cabbie rambled on about how for centuries, the Azeri people, the Shia Turks, and the Russians had tried to wipe the Armenians from the face of the earth; how his people's indomitable spirit would not succumb to those attacks; and how history would one day vindicate his people and restore them to their rightful place: the throne of the universe.

As all this unraveled, I couldn't help thinking about Frances, whose only wish was that history would remake her Czech people into a tenacious group, so that their powerful, belligerent neighbors could not have annexed them, as they had done in previous European conflicts.

As we crossed the bridge, and drove onto Flatbush Avenue, the cabbie finally came to the end of a winding statement about one or another virtue of the Armenians. I looked at him and nodded, to give him the impression that I had been listening all along.

"I'm telling you, my frien'," he continued. "The people of Turkey have a culture today because of us Armenians. They eat all the food we eat, they cook like us, they even look like us, but they don't like to hear that deep in their souls they ar' all Armenians. They want to kill that soul and remove it from their bodies. But how can you do that, my frien'?" he asked, with pompous laughter.

"Impossible," I said, shaking my head.

"You're right, my frien'. Impossible," he roared, absentmindedly veering out of his lane. The horns of cars riding alongside us screamed all at once, and were followed by curse words in Urdu, Creole-, Arabic-, Jamaican-, and African-accented broken English by fellow cabbies and other motorists. The Armenian collected himself and continued.

"Greece used to be Armenia. The people of ancient Greece and the whole area around it, all of them wer' Armenians."

"Hmn," I said.

"Incredible, right?"

I nodded.

I could tell that the Armenian was beginning to concentrate less and less on his driving and more on the history lesson he was bent on giving me. He looked at me often to make sure I was listening.

"And mor' than two thousand years ago in Sudan and Ethiopia, down in Africa, they wer' all Armenians."

Yeah, why don't you just say that the whole damn world was Armenia? I thought, and I wanted to tell the cabbie that I really didn't give a damn about his Armenian people—for the same reason that he, too, I was sure, didn't give a damn about the plight of black people. I wanted to tell him his very own mind-set was what caused whites to enslave blacks and the Turks to mistreat and dominate his Armenian people in the first place.

But all I could manage was, "I understand what you're saying, but what can one do about such human cruelties." He didn't respond, and to avoid the weird silence between us, I continued. "I mean, look at what America did to American Japanese and what the Japanese people also did to the Koreans during the Second World War; look at what white people did to us during slavery and colonialism; and even as you and I speak, the Israelis and the Palestinians are killing each other, the Serbians are killing the Bosnians, the Hutus are getting rid of the Tutsis, and so on and so forth. But such is the way of this world. Such is life." Aware that I was going off on a tangent, and also becoming uncomfortable that the cabbie uncharacteristically had not uttered a syllable the entire time, I stopped. When I looked at him, he appeared as if he was thinking hard about every word I had said.

He gave me a sideways glance and then began. "My frien', you said many, many important things." He paused. "But the most important thing you said is your question, 'What can one do about it?' "

"Yes, I mean, look at this country," I said. "When blacks speak about the reparation that is owed them, the whites tell them, 'fuhgettaboutit.' It's like saying: 'Yes, we treated you badly for centuries, but reality bites, life sucks, so get on with it.' " I was taken by surprise at how emotional I was suddenly getting.

"I understand what you ar' saying, my frien'," the cabbie started. He paused as he slowed down and prepared to make a left onto my street. "But you say human beings will always treat, er, other human beings badly and even kill them," he continued. "Now, let me give you an example. In the jungle, the tiger will never attack a lion or leopard for food. It attacks an animal that is not strong or doesn't know how to protect itself. So, unless the weak animal fights or gets strong, the tiger will always eat. Just the same in life, some people will always try to eat some people, but you have to make sur' you ar' not the one other people eat."

I was still chewing on what he had said when he started again.

"Because of what happened to my Armenian people, we have decided to never let that happen to us again. We ar' goin' to continue making noise and fighting back until we control our destiny. But, my frien', that is the problem I see with you blacks."

"How?" I asked.

"Because you keep quiet. Because you stop fighting. Because you ar' not hungry anymor'! Because you forgive. Your people making mistake, and if you'r' not careful, they will eat you again."

I was planning to attack the cabbie's theory by telling him that "irrespective of who dominates whom, humans are, in the end, mere pawns in the hands of history; and history uses us in the same way that we use donkeys to transport our gold, only to relieve them of the precious metals when we arrive at our destination." But the cabbie's last statement, which certainly contained some truth about my own people, forced me to remain quiet.

I looked out the window.

We were now on my block.

"It's building number 823," I said to him.

"Right or left side?" he asked.

"Right, toward the end of the block."

"No problem, my frien', but let me ask you one thing."

"Okay."

"You have heard of Zarathustra?" he asked as he pulled the cab in front of my building. He turned and faced me, our proximity so close that the air from his nose brushed against my forehead.

Fuck!

I had read Nietzsche's *Thus Spake Zarathustra* and other literature about the near mythical ancient prophet in a college ancient Greek philosophy course, but I still answered "No."

"Ahura Mazda was the first God, before God himself or even Zeus," the driver proclaimed. "And his prophet was called Zarathustra."

I nodded.

"And we Armenians, we still worship Ahura Mazda and his prophet Zarathustra," he continued. "And because he was from the Caucasus, we Armenians . . ." He paused for oratorical effect. "We Armenians are the true Caucasians and the true Aryans!" His tone was triumphant.

How the cabbie went from Zarathustra and his deity Ahura Mazda to the assertion that they, Armenians of the ancient Caucasus, were the true Aryans I wasn't quite sure, but afraid that any statement from me might spur him on I kept my mouth shut.

He suddenly turned quiet and contemplative, the olive skin of his forehead knit in a furrow. A few seconds passed without a word from him, and I remained transfixed on the seat. Then he smiled, reached below his seat, and gently pulled the lever of his car's trunk, which popped open immediately. I reached for my wallet, to pay for the ride, but the Armenian reached for my wrist and, looking into my eyes, said, "Don't worry, my frien', no fare for you." He smiled brightly, exposing a neatly arranged set of teeth, though they looked stained from cigarette smoking.

"Are you sure?" I asked.

"But, of course, of course," he said, continuing to smile.

Though I was uncomfortable with his gesture, I needed to hasten my exit from the cab. I said thanks and bowed my head. He printed out the receipt and handed it to me, saying, "You need this for taxes, no?"

"But you didn't have to do that," I said.

"Anything to help an artist."

Whatever.

With his chest resting on the steering wheel, the Armenian began fishing for something in a nook of his dashboard. After a few moments of searching, he produced a business card, which he handed to me. "You can call me anytime," he said, his eyes soft and moist.

"Thank you," I said, taking the card from him. The name on the card said just Sarkis.

"No problem, my frien'. In Armenia, the way we greet each other, we say, *Savat tanem.* So I am telling you, *Savat tanem!*"

I wasn't sure what to do next, though my instinct was to get out of the car immediately. But before I could make any move, Sarkis asked, "You know what that means, *Savat tanem?*"

"No," I said, wondering, How on earth am I supposed to know the meaning of *savat tanem?*

"*Savat tanem,* it means 'I'll take your pain.' "

I pondered for a few moments the profundity of what the man had just said. I extended my hand, which he took gladly and held in his for a good five seconds, his eyes peering into mine the whole time. I felt sympathy for the cabdriver. I wondered what life might have been for someone like him, who carried the heavy burden of his people's history in his heart and in his soul.

He seemed to nurse it like one nursed a sick bird, hoping that its wings would one day be strong enough for it to have another chance to soar in the skies.

The cabdriver released my hand. I realized that I hadn't told him my name when he told me his. But with one foot already on the street, I knew there was only one thing left for me to tell Sarkis. I looked into his eyes, and with a sudden deep respect said to the man, "I'll take your pain, too."

WARD G-4

When I was eight years old I realized, much to my own horror, that I had the odd gift of detecting death in people's eyes. It wasn't a gift I was particularly proud of, so I kept the horrible knowledge to myself, for fear of being branded as a dervishchild.

When Grandmother's brother, Baba Sala, fell sick, one look at him as he lay on his hospital bed in Ward G-4 of the Komfo Anokye Teaching Hospital, and I knew he wasn't going to live more than three days. And lo and behold, that was exactly how long Baba Sala lived. For three days and nights before his passing, I nursed the horrible thoughts brought on by my knowledge, wishing that the muses who had whispered the time of death were wrong. And when women came running into the courtyard, screaming, *Subhana Lillahi, Walhamdu Lillah,* breaking the news of Baba Sala's death, I somehow felt that I had had a hand in it. But then, I had often heard it being repeated that "there is no medicine for death." Whether I told anyone or not, Baba would die.

At the madrassa I was taught that up in Heaven, there exists a very large tree whose leaves bear the names of all the humans on this earth; and that at the approach of death, the color of the leaf bearing a person's name changes from green to yellow, eventually wilting and falling off the tree's branches. The Angel of Death, Azará-il, who checks for fallen leaves every morning, picks them all up and delegates his messenger angels to go down to earth to take the lives of the people whose names are on the leaves. Baba Sala's leaf from the Tree of Life had been struck by the yellow color of Death.

Komfo Anokye Teaching Hospital, or KATH, was located in Bantama, a suburb northwest of the city of Kumasi. It was a gigantic edifice with dozens of little buildings that surrounded it, covering about half a square mile of space. But as much a place of healing as KATH was, I saw it as a place where sick people went to be finished off.

A number of people from Zongo Street who were taken to the hospital never returned. My cousin Labaran was taken there after he hit his legs against a post while playing football. He was admitted to Ward B-2, the children's ward, and I never saw his face again. It was the same story with my aunt Iya, who was admitted to the maternity ward, A-1, when she was having her seventh child. The child, a baby boy, was brought home without his mother, whom I have not seen since. I wondered if Azará-il had taken up residence in the hospital's dark and long corridors and had moved his Tree of Life into the garden behind the hospital—next to the buried sword and statue of Komfo Anokye, the eighteenth-century Ashanti priest who summoned a Golden

Stool from the skies to unite the many warring clans of his tribesmen.

When I was twelve I was admitted to Ward G-4, the Intensive Care Unit of the hospital, where patients with serious ailments such as stroke, hypertension, high fever, and jaundice were treated. What started as malaria symptons (high temperature, severe chills, nausea, and vomiting) quickly degenerated into an uncontrollable fever, turning my eyes into a yellowish color within days.

A regular malaria attack takes no more than six days to run its course—nausea, vomit, and diarrhea during the first three days, followed by intense chills and a dangerously high body temperature between the third and fourth days. And regardless of whether you went to a hospital or not, you began to feel better by the fifth day, when the entire body itched very badly, the reaction most people had to the quinine pills. The itchiness, however, which usually lasted for a day or so, was welcomed, for it signaled that the malaria had run its course.

On the first day Mother gave me some paracetamol and quinine pills, which she bought from Teacher, the drugstore proprietor on Zongo Street. But a couple of days later, the fever seemed to have gotten worse. Mother then took me to the Manhyia polyclinic, a much smaller hospital compared to the giant Komfo Anokye. The doctors prescribed the same paracetamol and quinine Mother had given me, along with a penicillin injection.

On the way back from the polyclinic, Mother and I made a stop at Teacher's drugstore, where she bought me some vitamin

B tablets, although the doctor hadn't prescribed them. On Zongo Street, even a child would lecture you about the benefits of the tiny yellow-colored vitamin tablets.

"If you had told me he had malaria, I would've given him the injection myself; you could have saved yourself money and the trek all the way to Manhyia," Teacher said to Mother when he learned we were just returning from the hospital.

"I didn't know you gave injections," Mother replied.

"I have everything over there," Teacher said, pointing to a tiny room in the back of the store. "There's nothing a doctor does that I cannot do. Next time, eh. Don't waste your time going to the hospital. And tell everyone in your house that I give injections now, injections for any type of sickness. And cheap, cheap, too," Teacher said, grinning. Mother and I took the vitamin pills and left, with her promising to bring me to Teacher the next time I was sick.

Teacher was neither a pharmacist nor a doctor. As implied by his name, he was a middle-school teacher. But a nephew of his who lived in London and decided to invest in the pharmaceutical business had appointed Teacher, who was then an instructor at the Roman Catholic school, to operate the drugstore for him. And no sooner had Teacher started selling drugs than he began to administer prescriptions to his customers. Eventually he took to wearing long white coats, like those of a real medical doctor, and soon afterward, Teacher started giving injections, taking on the multiple roles of nurse, doctor, and pharmacist. From abdominal pains to headache, Teacher would convince his customers that they needed an injection, which he readily gave at a reduced price. "You can't have a strong injection without a strong medicine like *koday* to balance it," Teacher would tell the naive customers, to whom he would sell a week's dosage of codeine. "Call me a bastard, if you don't feel better in two nights," he would swear to his customers. Soon, we even heard that Teacher performed abortions in his back room, using a combination of Alafia herbal bitters and some unknown concoction he produced himself. We began calling him Doctor Teacher and regardless of whether Teacher was a quack or not, the people on Zongo Street swore by his diagnoses and prescriptions. And even though a few people had died after receiving doses of Teacher's potent medications, he was never implicated or shunned by the streetfolks, who believed, "Only Allah is capable of taking a life."

Amidst all the medical malpractice that went on in his back room, Teacher's business continued to prosper until the country's June 4, 1979, revolution, led by Flt. Lt. J. J. Rawlings. A horde of soldiers had descended upon Teacher's store and had beaten Teacher until his albino skin had turned black like ours. The soldiers, who carried machine guns and hand grenades, cleared the drugstore of every item, including the cash register and all the needles and bottles of codeine and paracetamol. Then they flogged him some more just to feel satisfied with themselves, before they carried Teacher and their loot away in their lorries and trucks. We never saw Teacher again after the incident, not even after the carnage of the revolution had died down a few months later and J. J. had returned political power to a popularly elected civilian government.

. . .

Like everyone else on Zongo Street, Mother believed that medicines worked twice or thrice faster if the dosages were increased two or threefold. So as soon as we got home, Mother gave me two codeines to chew, though Teacher had instructed her to give me only one pill, three times daily. Mother then prepared some dried adwene pepper soup for me, but I vomited it all out as soon as I had finished eating. She also gave me two vitamin B capsules, saying, "These will help you to eat more."

I was very nauseated, and food was the last thing I wanted. My head began to spin, and the next thing I knew, I was fast asleep. Moments later I heard Mother crying next to me. She mumbled something about her "Professor"—the nickname Mother proudly called me sometimes—dying. She cursed under her breath and lamented that she wished Father, who was traveling on a business trip to Nigeria, was home. Then Mother quickly wiped the tears from her face, as if she was embarrassed that I had caught her crying.

"Yaro, how do you feel?" she inquired, sobbing.

"I am feeling cold," I replied, my body shaking from the fever. My skin felt as if it had been submerged under a freezing pond, though my body temperature was as hot as a stove top. My teeth rattled and my ears hurt.

Mother dashed into the bedroom and came back with two big blankets that she wrapped around me. But that did nothing to stop the chills, which got progressively worse. She placed her right palm on my forehead and suddenly got alarmed. She ran out of the room and, moments later, returned with Mma Zakiya, her best friend and next-door neighbor. Soon afterward, Grandmother followed Mother and Mma Zakiya into the room. They both touched my forehead and exclaimed, "Wai, wai, wai. This is too much." Without a word to Mother and her friend, Grandmother bolted out of the room. She returned a few minutes later with a bottle of *jiko*, a concoction of mim tree bark, camphor, cloves, alligator pepper, and other mysterious medicinal herbs soaked in water. She poured a handsome amount of the drink in a little plastic cup and offered it to me. I drank the concoction slowly and made a face because of its bitter, unpleasant taste.

"Don't give him anything else for now," Grandmother instructed. "This will help strengthen his stomach, so he doesn't vomit. It's also very powerful against *ibba*." She exited the room, leaving Mother and Mma Zakiya to stand over me like guardian angels. Within minutes I was in another daze. I couldn't tell if I was asleep or awake. My body felt very light, and my ears were filled with a droning sound. I couldn't tell how long I was in this state, but when I opened my eyes it was morning, and Uncle Usama was standing like a giant in our living room. Uncle Usama was my father's junior brother, and was so tall that whenever he entered our chambers, he had to lower his head and bend his back, or else his head would hit the top of the door frame. He, too, touched my forehead to feel my temperature. And like the three women before him, Uncle Usama also concluded I had fever. He didn't say if it was "malaria" or "yellow" or any other kind of fever; he just said I had "*ibba*." Then Uncle Usama instructed Mother to prepare some milo and bread for me, and told her he would return in about half an hour to take me to the hospital.

While Uncle Usama was gone I vomited what little milo and

bread Mother had managed to feed me. Weak with hunger and nausea, I could barely sit upright. When Uncle returned, he andtwo boys helped me to walk to the Roman Hill taxi station, where he chartered a taxi to take us to the Komfo Anokye Hospital.

At the outpatient section of the hospital, a long queue had formed in front of the doctor's consultation room. Uncle immediately pulled the security guard aside and said a word or two in his ears, handing him a brown envelope during their short exchange. A few minutes later, I watched as the guard pulled a nurse aside and handed her the same brown envelope Uncle had given him. The guard also whispered something to the nurse and pointed in our direction. Then the nurse walked into the consulting room and, after a brief moment, walked outside and winked at the guard, signaling him to bring me in to see the doctor. With the assistance of another nurse, the guard escorted me into the consultation room. Uncle Usama followed.

As we entered the doctor's room, the people ahead of me in the queue shouted obscenities at the nurse and demanded to know why I was allowed to see the doctor so soon, when some of them had been standing in the queue since the break of dawn. "Is his sickness better than ours? Or his blood superior to ours?" an irate patient shouted after the nurse.

"God will punish you people for your bribery and corruption!" screamed another man.

"Don't mind those jealous people," the nurse whispered to Uncle once we were inside. She hurriedly took my temperature and pulse, and then opened an inner door for me to walk in and see the doctor, who was a well-fed, round-faced man who looked to be in his forties. The doctor's examination didn't take too long. He was done in less than five minutes, and handed Uncle a prescription for us to fill when we got home. But as we were about to leave the office, everything began to spin around me.

"Thank you, doctor. Get up and let's go," I faintly heard Uncle's commanding voice. Next thing I knew I was falling, falling, falling. Uncle sprang forward and grabbed me just before I hit the floor. I went completely blank.

I came to just a little after three in the afternoon. When I opened my eyes, Mother was sitting on a steel chair next to my bed, looking disheveled and sad. One of my four sisters, Jazi-a, stood next to Mother; and both of them smiled at me. I smiled back, happy to see them. There was a sudden sharp pain in my right arm. I looked toward my arm only to see a needle stuck there. And hanging from a metal stand next to my bed was a plastic drip container, whose contents were fed into my body through a tiny tube that was connected to the needle. There was another rubber tube below my nose, and a couple of plasters—Band-Aids—on my cheeks. My head ached as if I were being hit repeatedly with a hammer. And all around me sick, mostly old, people lay motionless on their beds. Mother and Jazi-a kept smiling at me, as if to assure me that everything was fine.

No sooner had it struck four on the ancient-looking clock on the facing wall than a throng of people rushed into the ward. Within seconds, my bedside was besieged by about as many as thirty people, each bearing a food gift of some sort, an age old, citywide tradition. Some of them just handed me money, for which Mother thanked them profusely. A few of my playmates and cousins and nieces were among the visitors, and I was so happy for all the attention that I almost forgot about my sickness. My headache subsided, and the feverish chills seemed to have gone. But soon a nurse came ringing a bell, announcing: "All visitors must leave the ward in ten minutes." One by one, all the people gathered at my bedside said good-bye to me and left. By five o'clock, the only people left were Mother, Grandmother, Uncle Usama, Jazi-a, and my three other sisters and three brothers. The nurse, who happened to be the head nurse during the night shift, made her final announcement, and demanded that everyone leave immediately. Mother gave the nurse some evaporated milk, sugar, and two tins of sardines—a bribe of sorts for her to take special care of me during the night. As Mother and the rest of the family got ready to leave, I started crying.

"Not to cry," said Mother. "I will be here first thing tomorrow morning, before you even wake up."

I continued to cry, bawling like a baby.

"What do you want me to get for you tomorrow morning?"

"I want you to bring me Baba's pocket radio," I replied, and ceased sobbing. I knew I was asking for a little too much and pushing my luck a bit far, as Father was inseparable from his pocket radio. It kept him abreast of local and world news in the mornings and early evenings. I had wanted Father's shortwave 1 transistor radio ever since he had brought it from Lagos some two or three trips ago; but he had refused to give it to me, claiming that I would break it. I actually didn't think Mother would go against Father's wish and give me the radio, but she was the one who asked me to name what I wanted, and there wasn't a better opportunity. Without affirming whether she would bring the radio or not, Mother and Jazi-a said good-bye to me and left.

Later that evening I met two of the patients in my section of the ward. To the right of my bed lay an old, bald-headed man who constantly griped about severe pains he felt in his left foot. Later on in the evening he told me gory stories about his "diyabitis sickness," and how he was waiting for the doctors to amputate his leg. To my left was another old man, gray-haired with deep sunken eyes, who complained of chest lacerations as his main ailment. He tried to make my acquaintance as soon as the doctor had finished his routine examination and left for the night.

"Say, *akwada*, what are you doing here?" he asked.

"I have fever."

"*Akwada*, you have feeba? But why did they bring you here? This is no place for small sickness like feeba, you know." I was scared and confused by what the old man said, and so I kept quiet. But he was relentless. "I see that you have lots of people; that's nice they brought you lots of food," he said and pointed his chin toward the top of my cupboard. It then occurred to me that there wasn't anyone at his bedside during the visiting hour.

"Yes," I said to him. "Do you want something to eat?" I asked.

"You bet I do, if you give me some," he said, and looked left and right, as if on the lookout for someone. "Hey, *akwada*," he said in a hushed tone, still looking around him. "Call the nurse and tell her you want to give me some food, but don't tell her I asked you for it."

I shouted for the head nurse, whose name was Felicia. She

hollered back from the middle of the ward that she would be on her way promptly. The old man, who I later discovered was suffering from heart disease, lifted his head from his pillow and said to me, "Let her give me some oranges, a boiled egg, a big slice of bread, and a tin of sardines. And remember, don't tell her I asked you, okay?"

The nurse frowned her face when I asked her to give him the food. "Listen, don't take away the boy's food, O! you good-for-nothing old man," she yelled at him.

"But, Madam *Nursee*, why are you cursing at me?" countered the old man. "Me, I don't like that, O! I didn't ask the boy; he himself took pity on me and decided to give me some of his food."

"Liar, liar," shouted the nurse. "How did he know you've been abandoned and all that? This boy was admitted only this morning." A sneer on her face, she sounded quite unfriendly.

"But he has eyes," countered the old man, who seemed angry now. "My suffering needs not be told; even a blind man can see it."

"*Ese wo ara,*" said the nurse and sucked her teeth in disdain. She dumped the food items on top of his empty cupboard, which looked as if it hadn't been cleaned in weeks.

"Don't mind her," the old man said of the nurse as soon as she was beyond earshot. "She wants all your food for herself, too. That's why she is *nicenice* to you, believe me, *akwada*! I have been here long enough to know all their tricks, these nurses. There isn't a single worthy one among their lot, I tell you!" He then took a big bite of the bread, which he dunked in the tin of sardines. He ate in silence and didn't look in my direction the whole time. I closed my eyes and fell into a deep slumber.

Mother was back in the ward by 5:15 A.M., almost an hour before the official morning visiting time, during which time only close relatives were allowed to bring food and other supplies to the sick folks. And to my biggest surprise, Mother handed me Father's tiny camouflage-colored transistor radio. I immediately switched it on and set the dial to GBC 2, the international section of the Ghana Broadcasting Corporation. The early-morning music program was in progress, but the reception was so poor that the announcer's voice sounded as if he were talking through his nose.

The doctor came in around ten o'clock and proceeded to make his usual rounds to each patient's bed. He instructed the nurses to put me on another drip when the current one was finished, making it the third since my admission. I had increased the drip's speed in the middle of the night, hoping it was the last one.

Even more people came to see me during the afternoon visiting hour, when Mother told me she had received message that Father was on his way home from Nigeria. The news of Baba's impending arrival brought a smile to my face. It left me giddy and happy all afternoon. I was so excited that I had problems falling asleep later in the evening. I eventually gave up and sat on the bed. I wanted to turn on the radio, but resisted doing so, because I knew it would disturb my neighbors.

The old man to my right—the one with the bad leg and "diyabitis"—was still awake, mumbling to himself. The one to my left was fast asleep. His loud snores created an eerie feeling amid the deep nocturnal silence of the ward. I couldn't tell if the patient directly across from me—whose name, I was told, was Boniface—was asleep or not. In fact, I hadn't seen his face since I came to the ward, and therefore didn't know what he looked like. His bed resembled a large mound, inside which a turbulent activity went on. His entire body had been encased in a brown blanket, and the only thing that gave any indication that a human being lay inside the mound was the sound and movement caused by his heavy breathing.

Spooked, I covered my head with the blanket. The old man to my right continued to mumble to himself. Then he suddenly started talking to me.

"*Akwada*, are you listening? Or you are asleep?" I pretended I didn't hear him. I closed my eyelids and succeeded, somehow, in forcing myself to sleep.

I woke up four hours later and immediately pushed the blanket from my face to inspect the ward. I saw Boniface for the first time; he sat up on the bed, his back hunched and his head bowed toward the center of his body, as if in meditation. I quickly pulled the blanket over my face. A few minutes later, when I slowly pushed away the blanket to steal a second glance at Boniface, he still sat upright, his eyes trained in my direction, as if he had deliberately waylaid my gaze in order to lock his eyes with mine. But I knew what he was up to and refused to stare at him directly. I looked at him from the corner of my eye, catching only the left side of his face. He looked to be in his seventies—white-haired and round-faced, with bulging, comical eyes.

"Look here," he called out. Reluctantly, I turned and faced him. And to my horror I saw *her* as soon as our eyes met. She, Death, was sitting comfortably in Boniface's dull eyes, ready to devour his soul. The Hausas, my tribe, ascribe the feminine gender to Death, though I never did learn the reason why.

"*Akwada*, what are you doing here?" Boniface asked. I was shocked by the strength of his voice. At first speechless, I finally managed to answer him. "I am sick," I said, looking aslant at him.

"I know . . . but this place is not for sick children," he said, his voice suddenly turning hoarse. "This place is for people nearing the tail end of their journey."

Tail end of their journey? What journey? Am I on a journey? From Zongo Street to the hospital? And then where?

I averted my eyes from his and instead gazed at the drip, which dropped slowly into the thin tube that ferried the liquid into my body.

"Don't sleep in this house another night," said the old, mysterious man, his gaze still turned on my eyes. "You are too young to be with us." Then he gently slid himself under his thick blanket, re-creating the familiar large mound.

Am I going to die, too? I wondered. I covered my body with the blanket and listened to Boniface's heavy, loud breathing. Not a wink of sleep crossed my eyes for the rest of the night. Meanwhile the old diabetes patient continued with his incoherent babble. And with the slow, creaky noise of the ceiling fan, the ward felt like a haunted house.

. . .

"When am I going home?" I asked Mother as soon as she walked in at dawn the next day.

"I don't know, but the nurse just told me the doctor wants to talk to me this morning. I'll ask him then."

"Good," I said, heaving a huge sigh.

"What is wrong, Yaro?" Mother asked.

For a brief moment I thought of telling her about what Boniface had said to me, but I knew the story wouldn't end there. She would want to know more. And I certainly didn't plan on telling her about my ability to see Death in people's eyes. Luckily for me, the man with chest lacerations lying next to me interrupted us when he *dropped his mouth* into our conversation.

"*Anti Ewuraba*, is that your son?"

"Yes," Mother replied, smiling.

"He is a good boy."

Mother continued smiling, not knowing that the old man was merely sweet-talking her into giving him some food.

"Tell the doctor about his chest pains, and, *Ewuraba*, let them keep the boy and treat him well, well," he continued.

Mother was baffled. She looked at me quizzically.

"Chest pains? I didn't know . . ."

"No, Mma. I don't have any chest pains. *Karya ya keyi, abinci yake so*," I added in our Hausa tongue—which the old man didn't understand—to tell Mother that the old man was lying and that he was just trying to keep me in the ward longer so he could continue to get food from us. Later that afternoon a nurse informed us that the old man had been in the ward and in the same bed for the past three months, and that the hospital authorities had been trying to get rid of him, but no family member or relative would come forward to pay his medical bills, which kept accumulating.

The doctor came to my bedside around 10:15 A.M., and immediately asked the day nurse to stop the drip after the one I was to finish. He took Mother aside and spoke to her for a few minutes. He signed some papers and examined me once again, and then left my bedside without telling me if I would be discharged that day or not. I was so saddened and frightened by the thought of spending another night in the ward that I began to cry.

"Why is he crying?" the nurse, who was just about to give me my morning dose of pills and injections, inquired of my mother.

"I want to go home," I cried, unable to control myself.

"How is his chest? *Ei, akwada,* how is your chest pains?" chimed in the old man.

"Shut up your mouth. Who begged for your wisdom?" barked the nurse. The old man didn't say a word more. I kept crying. Mother asked me to compose myself and act like a grown-up. I cried even louder.

"But you are discharged. Doctor says here you can go home this evening," said the nurse, pointing at a sheet she was perusing.

I stopped crying immediately.

Mother thanked the nurse and gave her four cans of milk, a packet of sugar, and a half-dozen fresh eggs. She also gave the man with the lacerated chest some sardines, bread, and fresh oranges. He thanked Mother and insisted she should be watchful of my chest pains. "*Yakare kanka*," Mother retorted in our language, implying that the old man's bad wishes would fall on his head. I was so excited about the news of my discharge, I forgot to ask Mother if she had heard anything more from Father. I was already imagining myself in my home clothes, waving good-bye to the two old men as I left the ward after that evening's visit.

The drip needle was removed from my arm not long after Mother left. I took advantage of the freeing of my hand and walked to the lavatory without the nurse's assistance. I avoided looking at the lavatory mirror, afraid I might see Death in my own eyes. I left the lavatory in a hurry and returned to my bed. I tried to catch GBC 2 on the radio, but all I heard was a breezy sound and an occasional scratchy voice that was barely audible. I turned my back to the ward and faced the window, from where I watched the sprawling city of Kumasi, with all its magnificient hills and valleys. I could see as far as Roman Hill, Zongo Hill, the Kumasi Central Market, and even Tech, the farthest point south of the city.

I must have been looking outside for quite a while and become completely lost in my thoughts, because when I turned to look back to the ward, I caught sight of the tail end of a covered steel stretcher being pushed out of the hall by two men in white gowns and gloves. They also wore white patches that covered their nostrils. I looked across the room, toward Boniface's bed. Both he and his great mound were gone. The bed had been stripped of all the sheets and blanket and pillow. I knew instantly that the old man's leaf had fallen off the Tree of Life, which could mean only one thing: the Angel of Death had visited the ward and was perhaps still hanging around, looking to take more lives.

All morning and afternoon I avoided looking toward the dead man's bed. Mother arrived at three-thirty and was accompanied by Father. After asking how I was, Father pulled a rectangular orange-and-blue box from the side pocket of his *crimplin* jacket and handed it to me. When I opened it, the box contained a portable transistor radio of the same color as the box. I cried with joy, and immediately tried to find GBC 2. The reception this time was far clearer than it was with the other radio. "*Maye Hot*" ("I Am Feeling Hot"), the most popular highlife music of the time, performed by Eddie Donkor, was playing, with the presenter's voice in the background. I was consumed with joy, and the thought of how the kids at school would find my brand-new radio hip and cool. I smiled to myself, switched off the radio, and said to Father, "Thank you."

Rachmaninov

The School of Visual Arts was having an art opening to celebrate the end of the summer session, and a former college classmate was showing his work. So Felix, both as a show of support for his friend and also to check out what all the enrolled artists were producing, headed to Twenty-first Street on Manhattan's West Side, where, as usual, he was one of three or four blacks milling among the crowd.

He found his friend, whose name was Zach, and joined the loose conglomerate of his friends, friends of friends, and casual associates, and for the rest of the show, and even an hour or so afterward, the nine of them hung out in the gallery's makeshift reception area, shooting the shit and jockeying for position next to the ones in whom they had more than a passing interest. A 1.5-liter bottle of Concha y Toro was passed around the group, and each one of them took a turn gulping down voluminous swigs. After a while the group was broken up into two smaller parties, one of which included Zach, his ex-girlfriend, Amanda, and three other guests, a man and two women, whom Felix had not met yet.

Felix was in the company of Christina, Daisy, and Zoot.

Zoot was an intentionally weird-looking guy of about twenty-six, with thick sideburns and a smoothly shaved head and eyebrows. Felix was almost a hundred percent sure that "Zoot" was not the name the man's parents had christened him with. Christina was a green-eyed brunette of medium height and a shy demeanor, and it was the third time Felix had seen her—the other times were at art openings as well. Felix had been attracted to Christina since their first meeting, but the two had never had the chance to speak intimately to each other. This could be the night, Felix thought, for me to make a move on her. Felix was quite convinced that Zoot had his eyes on Daisy, who was similarly weird-looking. She sported tattoos of various colors and shapes on her neck, arms, and her well-exposed cleavage. Daisy also had a pierced tongue and a pierced belly button, both of which were adorned with silver rings. She opened her mouth widely when she spoke, as if to draw people's attention to the contraption in her mouth. Felix had caught Zoot staring at Daisy's cleavage or exposed belly a good six times since they started talking. The party's idle chatter was developing into a "deep" discussion about social issues. And, as usual, Felix was doing most of the talking.

"This is what I suspect," Felix was saying. "Rich people avoid discussing money with their poor friends for four reasons." He dangled his right fist and, starting with the thumb, pulled out a finger each time he made a point. "One, they are in constant fear of being asked monetary favors; two, they feel guilty for their wealth in the midst of poverty; three, they don't want to appear vain; and four, they want to be liked or respected because of who they are and not because of their money." Christina nodded reluctantly, with a skeptical look on her face. Daisy, with knit-browed bohemian pensiveness, stared keenly at Felix, apparently in complete agreement with him.

"Totally, man, I hear that. God, that's what they do," said Zoot.

"Yes, you see, even these four reasons I gave you are only the sub-reasons why rich people don't like discussing money. The overriding factor, the real and inner motive behind their aversion, is miserliness. They simply don't want to part with their money." The women's reaction was the same as before, and Zoot, who was still in agreement, shouted, "Totally, man, and that's why they keep getting richer."

"I tell you, man, that's the bottom line," Felix added and paused to look at a woman who had just joined them from the other party. She was tall, slender, blue-eyed, and dirty blonde.

"Almost every rich person I know is a cheapskate," he continued. "The majority of the students at my college were wealthy trust-fund babies, or what I call TFBs, with hundreds of thousands, and even millions, in their trust-fund accounts, yet they constantly complain they are broke, as if they wanted to stand in solidarity with me, with my not being one of them, you know. And this is what pissed me off even more: they bummed cigarettes off me, though they knew I could hardly afford a pack."

"Where did you go to college?" asked the tall, blue-eyed woman, who smoked continuously during Felix's spiel about his alma mater.

"Southampton College," he replied.

"Hmn," she said, squinting, as if attempting to deduce something from his short answer.

"Yeah, but don't mistake me for one of those TFBs; I was there on scholarship," said Felix.

"You guys want to do something, maybe go somewhere and have a drink?" Zoot asked suddenly as if he were bored with the conversation. "I know a place just a few blocks from here." The group jumped at Zoot's idea, and soon after left the art gallery.

Felix was brooding on the way to the bar. He resented the way that Zoot had cut short the exchange between him and the dirty blonde. The group had split into three parties as they walked, but had all come together at the traffic light. The blonde, as if waiting for the opportunity, moved closer to Felix.

"Hi, my name is Greta," she said, and extended her hand just as the light flicked to green.

"Felix," he said and shook her hand, faking a smile. As they walked, Felix quickly sized her up, and calculated that Greta was about an inch taller than he was. He was five-nine.

"So, I heard you are an artist, too," she said, smiling and taking a long drag of her cigarette.

"How did you know that?" he asked, half smiling, loosening up a bit.

"I have my sources."

"Cool, cool," Felix said, twisting his wild-looking dreadlocks, which were down to his shoulders. "I see, so whose work did you come to see?" he asked.

"Pat, do you know him?"

"Nope."

"He's the one in the blue Yankee cap. I'll introduce you two when we get to the bar."

"Cool," he said, bobbing his head up and down.

"I met him through Amanda," she added.

"Oh, so you're friends with Amanda?"

"Oh, yeah! We've been friends since childhood," she replied, puffing smoke out of her mouth.

"Really?"

"We went to the same elementary school in Chicago."

Felix's eyes trailed Christina's actions and movements, waiting for the perfect moment to approach her.

"Amanda told me you're from Africa," Greta continued.

"What else did she tell you about me?" he asked in mock seriousness.

"Not much, but she told me you are from Ghana."

"Yep."

"So, how was it growing up in Ghana?"

"It was okay, I guess. But I couldn't wait to leave and go to college," Felix said.

"So, you probably don't go back to visit, do you?"

"I've been back only once," Felix answered, shrugging his shoulders. "How long have you been in the city?" he asked her, in an effort to deflect her questions.

"About three months, I just graduated from Sarah Lawrence."

"Right on! And what are you planning to do with your life?"

"I'm going to take the year off and relax, you know, do some traveling while I wait to hear from Columbia."

"Great," Felix said as they approached the entrance to the bar.

He held the door open for Christina, and as she walked in, his eyes traveled the length of her slender body, zooming in on her wide hips and long legs. Though Greta was very attractive, Felix didn't think they were each other's type. He liked quiet, reserved women like Christina; extroverted and overly confident "chicks" like Greta were not his cup of tea. They disturbed the mental equilibrium he tried to maintain in his life. And moreover, erotically, he was more drawn to curvaceous women with ample booties.

The light was dim inside O'Kelly's. The bar area was crowded with partygoers, some engaged in exuberant conversations, while others just stood near the bar, sipping their drinks and listening to the loud music that came from the overhead speakers. A waitress came by and informed the group that there weren't any empty tables, not even in the large dining section down in the basement. Still, the group decided to stay and have just one drink, and then either move on to a different bar in the neighborhood or move the party uptown, to Greta's apartment.

Felix became sort of detached from the group when they entered the bar. Though he contined talking to Greta, he refused to say a word when the others deliberated about moving the party elsewhere. But he more than anyone else would have appreciated leaving the crowded joint. He actually contemplated leaving the bar and returning to Park Slope, where he was cat-sitting for Kirk, a musician friend of his who was on a two-week

West Coast tour with his band. Felix didn't have an apartment of his own; he shared a loft space with two other artists in the deserted Brooklyn waterfront neighborhood located down under the Manhattan and Brooklyn Bridge overpass, known as DUMBO. Though the studio was rented as a work-only space, Felix had moved in a few of his belongings, including a futon bed, and spent his nights there, right beside giant canvasses and in the obnoxious smell of paint, oil, and industrial dust. House- or catsitting for his friends was, therefore, an opportunity for Felix to return to civilization, away, if only temporarily, from the hum of industrial machinery; the rattling sound of the D, Q, and B trains crossing the Manhattan Bridge; the noise of vehicular traffic; and finally, the rabies-infested stray dogs that almost outnumbered the die-hard artists who were bent on evicting the four-legged creatures and establishing an artist colony.

As a self-imposed rule, Felix avoided going to clubs or joints above Union Square. He called the area of Manhattan above Fourteenth Street "white town," where he believed he attracted mean stares from jealous white boys who became filled with disdain the moment they saw a black guy with a Caucasian woman. Felix, therefore, felt more at home in the East Village and the Lower East Side or in Brooklyn, where he mingled with fellow artists and musician friends, though all of them were white as well. He planned to write a book on the topic of his isolation, which he would call, *The Social Isolation of the Black Artist at the End of the Second Millennium.* In this book, Felix would analyze the pathological and psychological factors behind the isolation many black artists like himself impose on themselves, and would trace its roots to the indifferent reception black artists receive from their own people, the main catalyst to their isolation, and why they tend to gravitate toward whites, who patronize and support them and their art.

Felix always kept a notebook in which he wrote down his polemic and fiction ideas and even outlines of the many books he would write in the near future. He planned, or rather fantasized, on retiring his brushes after making it big in the city, and would then devote the rest of his life to writing books of essays on race, culture, and *The Sexual Complexity and Supremacy of the Blacks*—a topic he had often thought of. Usually the token lone and cool black dude among his artist, musician, and actor friends, Felix thought he had observed and gathered enough material and information about the "dull" sexual nature of white men to write a polemic that, by means of "juxtaposition and counterposition," would reveal to the world why the African is not only superior, but a highly complex sexual being.

"So, what did you study at Sarah Lawrence?" Felix asked Greta.

"Math and philosophy."

"Damn, are you serious?"

"You bet. I double-majored."

"You think you gonna get a job with those degrees?" Felix asked, with a smirk on his face.

"I really don't need one at this point," she said, and looked in his eyes as if searching for a specific reaction.

"You fucking with me, right? How are you going to pay rent?"

"I own my apartment," she answered nonchalantly and added, "I guess that makes me a TFB, right?"

"Oh," he responded, slightly taken aback.

"Don't worry about it," she said, giggling.

Just then a waitress approached the group and announced that a table in the basement would be ready for them in about fifteen minutes. They quickly decided to take it, since most of them were hungry and therefore wanted to stay and order some food.

"Hey, anyone wanna go out and have some fresh air with Daisy and me before we eat?" Zoot asked.

The replies of "Yeah," "Sure," "Sounds great," and "Right on" came from Zach, Amanda, Greta, and Felix respectively.

Christina and the other two people decided they didn't need fresh air. Zoot searched for the waitress and asked her to inform Christina when the table became available. They walked out and walked west, toward Eighth Avenue.

Zoot began to roll a joint, with his eyes still on Daisy's chest. The weather had cooled off just a bit from the day's oppressive heat. The pavement was crowded with groups of boisterous people walking to or from a show, a bar, or a restaurant. And there were the evening strollers, couples walking hand in hand, engrossed in each other's company.

Along the way the group found a poorly lit storefront with a huge garbage container beside it. "Let's stop here," Zoot said to the group. He produced a lighter from his pocket and lit the joint. He took a long drag and passed it along. Felix was amazed by how much of a pro Greta was with the joint; she wasted no smoke, taking every bit of the drag straight into her lungs, without coughing even once.

Felix liked the sedate but powerful feeling pot gave him, and believed that he would've definitely turned into a pothead if he had money to buy the stuff on a regular basis. Almost all his friends in the city did hard drugs like ecstasy and coke on top of the seemingly less dangerous pot. Felix had never touched hard drugs in his life. That shit is for white folks, he would say to himself. But he saw nothing wrong with smoking pot, and was even convinced of its medicinal and spiritual values.

The joint was finished in no time and, surprisingly, Greta asked if anyone wanted another. "Sure," everyone chorused. She pulled a small stash from her pocket and handed it to Zoot, who smelled it and exclaimed, "Shit, this smells great!" She smiled and said, "I have my sources." Zoot rolled a smaller one this time, and returned the remainder of the stash to Greta. She put it in her pocket and, moving closer to Felix's face, whispered in his ear, "You and I can smoke the rest later."

"Right on," he whispered back, smiling, though quite surprised by her move. He had been under the impression that Greta hated his guts for speaking the way he did about TFBs.

"What are you two whispering about?" Amanda prodded.

"Nothing," Greta retorted.

"Whatever," Amanda said.

The six were very stoned by the time they returned to the bar. The waitress guided them to their table, and they immediately began ordering dinner. Everyone, with the exception of Felix, ordered an appetizer and a dinner plate. Being perpetually broke and only with about eighteen dollars in his pocket, Felix ordered just a bowl of soup. In a rather unexpected move, Greta asked for the wine list, from which she ordered a bottle each of Merlot and Pinot Grigio. "Wine's on me, guys," she said as she handed the list to the waitress. "Thanks," the group responded. Still, some, including Greta, ordered mixed drinks as they waited for the food to arrive. Felix didn't order anything else, and kept guzzling the water in the pitcher in front of him.

Two hours later, after the lethal combination of wine, beer, and Captain Morgan and Cokes, Greta was quite intoxicated and high. And so was Felix. The two chatted almost exclusively, and casually patted and touched each other on the knees in drunken excitement.

In all of Greta's twenty-three years of life it was the first time she had found herself in such intimate proximity to a black guy. While growing up, she was into Hendrix, Nina Simone, Diana Ross, Prince, and a host of other black artists, and was generally fascinated by American blacks and their culture. This fascination had eventually turned into a semi-obsession with the black male body, largely due to her love of basketball and her hometown hero, Michael Jordan.

"I love Michael Jordan," she said in reaction to Felix's mention that basketball was the only sport he had any interest in.

"You gotta love the guy. I mean, he is the greatest ever to play the game."

"Oh, I just love him, he is so beautiful," Greta emphasized, looking deeply into Felix's eyes. She leaned closer, and again whispered in Felix's ear. He nodded and the two suddenly got up and excused themselves from the table. "We'll be right back," Felix said to the group, and winked at his friend, Zach.

"Don't wait for us," Greta added, giggling as they walked away.

"Don't do what I won't do," joked Amanda. Zoot didn't even seem to notice the couple's departure. He was too engrossed in Daisy's cleavage to hear or notice anything.

As soon as they stepped out into the breezy night, Greta handed Felix the leftover pot she had kept in her pocket. "You wanna roll it?" she asked.

"Sure," he said and took the little sack from her. He removed the pot and a sheet of rolling paper and began to roll.

"So, how do you describe the kind of painting you do?" she asked, looking at Felix's precise facial features, the well-defined jawline and high cheekbones.

"To tell you the truth, I can't really describe what I do; I'm just a painter. All I can tell you is that the sole mission in my paintings is to document the human experience, especially as it pertains to the African and black American. In what specific form or style the work turns out is not for me to say or categorize. That is the responsibility of the so-called critics of art; that is what they are paid to do, right?" Felix paused, took a hit of the blunt, and passed it on to Greta.

"Wow," Greta said, and smoked voraciously.

The two had begun walking southward when they left the bar, without any specific idea as to where they were headed. They were now at Eighteenth Street and Seventh Avenue, and had just finished smoking the joint.

"What program are you applying for at Columbia?" Felix asked.

"The graduate writing program."

"Okay, now you're really fucking with me. You write, too? Now, don't tell me you are already published. I'll be really jealous."

She laughed hysterically. "No, as a matter of fact I've never sent anything out," she said. "I have been working on this one novel since my sophomore year, though I haven't told anyone about it. You're the first person, apart from my parents and grandparents, that I am telling this to."

"I see," came the curt response from Felix.

"Yeah, I know it's weird, but I actually consider myself more of a writer than anything else."

"That's deep. You know, I've been thinking . . . we have lots in common, you know," said Felix. "I write as well, and I have dozens of essays outlined and researched and ready for me to begin writing when the right time comes."

"What are some of the topics?"

"Well, mostly sociocultural analysis and political and social commentary focused on blacks in the diaspora," he said.

"But what exactly do you mean by that?" she asked.

"To be able to pinpoint black issues and to bring them out in the open, not only as a means of dealing with and solving our problems, but also as a means of educating the world about who we are as a people. Kinda like what DuBois did."

"Huh?" Greta said.

"You are familiar with DuBois's work, right?"

"Of course I am. But I was just thinking of how you are actually more of a thinker than a writer," she said.

"Perhaps."

The two were now almost in the heart of the West Village—at Twelfth Street and Seventh Avenue—and were beginning to get very comfortable and loose with each other. They were at a threshold and they each realized their few hours of friendship were about to become something more. Felix gently took Greta's hands, locking his fingers with hers. She didn't resist, and held and squeezed his hands tightly, as if to crack the bones of his lanky fingers. They stared into each other's eyes, unblinkingly, frozen by the power and sensuality of their passion. All of Felix's natural senses told him there wouldn't be a better time. And very slowly he pulled Greta closer to him until her face almost touched his. They jumped at each other, and began kissing and embracing in the middle of the street. People walked past them, some turning around after a few steps to look at them. They kissed nonstop for almost two minutes, and then moved from the street to the front of an unopened store and continued kissing.

For Greta it was as if her years of fantasizing about black men had finally congealed into one intense and irreversible desire to touch Felix, to feel him and see if his body was as lean as the bodies of those basketball players she saw on television. Throughout her college years and even back in her high school days, Greta had fantasized about dating a black guy, but circumstances had crippled that possibility. She went to a virtually all-white private high school in Chicago. And she was faced with the same situation during her years at Sarah Lawrence, where there were no men at all.

Though all of his friends were white, Felix had gone out of his way to try to date black women when he first moved to the city. But after three months, Felix succeeded in dating only one black woman, whose lifestyle and attitude was contrary to his own. Not only did she expect Felix to pay for everything when they went out to eat or see a movie, but she also acted like a queen bee, asking for everything and giving nothing in return. After the queen bee, most of the other black women Felix approached were either blatantly uninterested in him or seeing someone else. In the end, Felix felt he wasn't successful at dating black women because he wasn't black enough for them. Felix had therefore decided to go back to dating the white girls he was used to, though he hadn't been active in pursuing anyone for the past few months.

Felix abruptly pulled away from Greta and said to her, "Let's go to Brooklyn."

"Brooklyn? Is it safe?" she asked in a slur that, for the first time, gave away her drug- and alcohol-induced state. Felix, too, was high and intoxicated, and enjoyed every second of it.

"Don't be silly," Felix said.

Though Greta had gone twice to Yankee Stadium in the Bronx—the only place she had visited outside of Manhattan— she didn't like leaving her Upper West Side neighborhood. The outer boroughs seemed like faraway states or even countries to her.

"Come on, we are going to Park Slope," Felix persisted. She had a few friends who lived in that section of Brooklyn, and they always raved about their neighborhood.

"Yeah, that's cool. Let's go." She jumped forward and flagged an oncoming cab. The two jumped into the rear seat and immediately began kissing.

Kirk's apartment building was located a block and a half from Prospect Park.

When the couple finally managed to walk into the fourth-floor walk-up apartment, Felix lit a stick of Naag, his favorite incense. It soon filled the room with a powerful and hypnotic scent. Felix inhaled deeply. His senses were stirred by the strong, pungent smell, which was an aphrodisiac to him, arousing and inspiring him all at once to action.

Everything seemed new and exciting to Greta. The incense smell, Felix's aura, the mystique of his incense-oil-smelling dreadlocks, his blackness, his view on things, and lastly, his dedication to his art.

Kirk's two-bedroom apartment had a tiny boxlike living room and a bathroom and kitchen so small, two people could hardly fit inside comfortably. A couple of antique coffee tables sat in the corner of the living room, and there was also a worn-out reclining chair in the opposite corner. A makeshift wooden rack occupied most of the living room space; a stereo component, complete with amplifier, double-deck tape player, and phono player were arranged on the rack's upper shelves. The bottom shelf contained dozens of jazz, classical, and blues vinyl LPs. A window looked from the living room to a narrow alley that separated the building from the one to its right.

"How much do you pay for this place?" Greta asked Felix.

"Nothing. It's not my place. I'm catsitting for a friend of mine who is out in LA."

"Okay, now it makes sense; I was wondering about that, because Amanda told me you live in DUMBO."

"Yep, that's my neighborhood," Felix said, smiling. "Just a second," he said, and ran to the kitchen, which was fully stocked with liquor of all sorts. He returned with two glasses of gin—hers with tonic, lime, and ice, his straight.

"How is it down there in DUMBO?" Greta asked after taking a sip.

"Okay, if you don't mind living in dusty old factory buildings." They both laughed.

"Where is the cat you're supposed to be taking care of?"

"It's a very independent cat; doesn't like people that much," said Felix. "It's probably in the bedroom, take a look?" He opened the door to the dark bedroom, feeling for the light switch.

"Naaah, later. What's his name, or her name?

"Who?"

"The cat."

"Oh, his name is Zeus."

"Zeus. Must be one powerful cat."

"I guess."

After countless make-outs, noisy marathon kisses, and outlandish gyrations that led to an intense lovemaking session, the couple lay on the living room rug, naked and still intoxicated from all the alcohol they had consumed. Felix got into his under-wear and got up and walked to the kitchen. He returned with two cuts of lime, a glass filled with ice cubes, and a bottle of tonic water, with which he mixed some more gin and tonic for Greta. For himself, he poured a half glass of the gin, without tonic or ice cubes.

"A toast to decadence," Greta said.

"Let's find something to listen to," Felix said and crawled toward the rack. The first vinyl he grabbed had a blue-and-black cover with a picture of Stan Getz. The LP, titled *Getz Au Go Go*, was the 1964 live performance of the saxophonist, featuring As-trud Gilberto at the Cafe Au Go Go in New York's Greenwich Village. Felix thought it was a good choice, though he wasn't fa-miliar with Getz's music himself. While they listened, Felix opened the album's centerfold to read the information, and to his delight found a cache of a pot-looking substance in it. He showed it to Greta. "Can we smoke it?" she asked, hardly able to conceal her excitement at the find.

"I don't think Kirk will mind," Felix answered. He sniffed at the substance, as if to confirm its authenticity. It smelled like pot, all right, though it contained some unusual particles the nature of which Felix couldn't quite make out. Some looked like cat hairs; he picked them out one at a time. Then he ran to the bed-room and returned with a phalluslike bong whose water looked like it had been sitting in the contraption for weeks. But both were too drunk and too eager to take note of this. In a few mo-ments the bong's psychedelic belly was pregnant with an impres-sive array of smoke colors—ash, white, purple, blue, orange—of which the couple took turns inhaling.

They quickly smoked the batch and refilled their glasses with more gin and tonic. Felix toasted this time around. "To deepness," he said. He refilled the bong with the remaining pot, and asked Greta, "You want some more?" But there was no reply from Greta. She sat sullenly on the floor, with her arms crossed in front of her raised knees. Her eyes looked distantly into nowhere, her lips moved as if she were reciting a silent prayer.

"Are you okay?" Felix asked, alarmed.

"I'm fine," Greta answered.

"You don't look fine."

"Can you change the music, please? Put on something softer." Greta's voice was soft, broken, and full of fear. She got up and moved to the futon couch.

"But this is very soft," Felix insisted in a gentle voice.

"Will you please change it?" Greta sounded frustrated.

He found an old vinyl of Rachmaninov, titled *Rachmaninov Plays Rachmaninov*, and replaced the jazz album. Though the album was scratchy, the opening composition's brilliance—coupled with the warm rendition given it by its own author—shone through.

"That's much better," Greta said as soon as she heard the first notes of the Elegie in E-flat Minor, a slow-tempoed solo piano piece with a soothing yet haunting and repetitive melodic line. "Yeah, much, much better," she reiterated after a few minutes of listening to the piece with her eyes completely shut.

Felix, on the other hand, began panicking. He felt dizzy, especially when he closed his eyes. He slumped into the futon's deep womb, next to Greta. She looked like a nymph who had come to the end of her line, wasted, and wretched. Black spots appeared beneath her eyes, making her look ghoulish.

"Are you feeling anything?" Felix asked Greta, wondering if she was going through the same bizarre mental state as he was.

"I don't know how I feel. Maybe I'm just freaking out, and everything is just happening in my head."

"What do you mean?" he asked.

She looked at him strangely. "I don't know, but I still can't tell what's going on with me," she said and jumped from the futon, stepping away from Felix.

"Are you okay?"

"I think you should call the ambulance," she said.

"Why?"

"My heart is beating like hell. I feel like I'm going to die."

Felix tried to make eye contact with her, but she avoided his gaze.

"Look at me," he said, and grabbed her by the shoulders, forcing her to face him. Her eyes, though opened widely, didn't seem to have any spark in them. They stared unblinkingly at nothing.

"Are you going to call the ambulance? I feel like I'm going to die."

Felix wondered if he had heard the ambulance plea before or if he was just hearing it for the first time. Time seemed to be crawling. Worse, it also seemed to be going one step forward and three backward. He was quickly losing even the rudimental ability to measure or gauge anything. His mind floated in a cloudy vacuum in which time was free-floating; it stopped, moved backward, and tried to move forward again. Felix didn't have a watch and neither did Greta, so they had no means of telling how long it had been since they came to the apartment.

Meanwhile, Rachmaninov continued playing Rachmaninov. The needle of the old Technics SL-BD20 automatic turntable system, a contraption that looked like it was manufactured in the seventies, kept going back to the top of the record, repeating the pieces over and over and over, starting with the Elegie in E-flat Minor and ending with the last track, Humoresque in G Major, a brashly rendered piece with a rising and falling intensity and an intermittent melodic line. Felix wondered how many times the phono player had repeated each piece. Twenty? Twenty-five times? Maybe fifty? He thought he heard Greta repeat that she was going to die. Again, he wondered if she had actually said that, or was his mind just repeating what she had said a while ago? Felix just wasn't sure of anything at this point. He merely stared at his companion and did nothing.

Soon Greta began to cough and the coughs got progressively louder. She got up and paced around the room, holding her hands to her chest as if something was about to erupt from her breasts. Felix saw her mouth move, though he couldn't quite tell if she was speaking directly to him or not. With a valiant mental effort he shook his head almost violently and managed to jerk himself into the present. He rushed to the phone, picked up the receiver, and began to dial a number—389 . . . But he went blank, unable to remember the last four digits of the number. He gave it a fresh try, focusing more on the number buttons than on his memory. After a dozen or so tries he succeeded in dialing Jim's number. Jim was an electric-guitar player, a friend of both

Kirk's and Felix's, who lived a few blocks down with his painter girlfriend. He was a frank, no-nonsense type of a guy, a punk and heavy metal rocker whose attitude was just as loud and effusive as the music he played and listened to at decibels high enough to permanently damage one's eardrums.

"Yeah," Jim said in the typical way he answered the phone.

"Hey, Jim it's me, Fe—"

"Damn, are you wasted or something? You know what time it is?"

"What time is it?" stammered Felix in a low, frightened voice.

"Damn, homeboy must be really hammered! It's almost three, you know. Now, what can I do you for?"

In a few hurried sentences, mindful of the fact that his brain could freeze or even shift to reverse on him at any time, Felix told Jim what had happened.

"So, where is she now?" Jim asked, realizing the urgency of the situation. Jim had been a punk rocker since he was twelve, and therefore was not unfamiliar with people "losing it" or even dying of overdoses.

"She's right here."

"Felix, I feel like I am really going to die, are you talking to nine-one-one?" Greta managed to say before collapsing on the couch. Miraculously, Jim's perfect ears, despite the loud music in the background, picked up Greta's question.

"What the fuck, man. Is she okay?" he said from the other end.

"She actually isn't. She's lying on the couch and wants me to call nine-one-one . . ."

"Dude, DO NOT call nine-one-one, no matter how freaked

out she gets. You make the mistake of taking her to the emergency room and you gonna be in some deep shit; they're not gonna believe anything you tell them. They gonna think you doped her or something. Know what I mean? Is she black or white?

"She's this rich white chick, friend of Amanda, Zach's ex-girlfriend," whispered Felix, his lips closer to the mouthpiece.

"Yeah, yeah, yeah," interrupted Jim.

"And we just met tonight . . ."

"Dude, if I were you I would keep nine-one-one out of this. A loaded white chick gets fucked up on her first date with a black dude?"

"It's not a date. We just—"

"Doesn't matter, man. You see where I was heading, right? They gonna think there's something funny going on, I swear."

Greta made a painful, growling "unnh" noise.

"Are you okay?" Felix asked. He was still panicky himself.

"What the fuck, Felix! Are you listening to me?"

"Yes, yes,"

"Do whatever you need to do to wake her up, but keep EMS out of this. I am sure it's nothing big; she probably just had a bad high or a 'bad combination' something. Listen, make her some strong coffee or give her lots of oh-jay and then take her out for a walk, you know, to get some fresh air. I am sure that'll help. I don't know. Dude, I'd even suggest you give her a good fuck with that black mamba of yours!" Jim laughed hoarsely, thinking what he said was funny.

"What do you mean, give her a good fuck, she is fucking sick right now and looks like she is going to die!" Felix said, his body shaking.

"But it works, man. Trust me. Just give it to her."

Felix decided it was time he hung up the phone. Jim was a handyman who could fix and build almost anything he set his mind to, and Felix had expected him to somehow fix the situation for him; but judging from their conversation, he wasn't sure how Jim's handiness was going to be helpful to his situation with Greta. "Thanks, bro', I appreciate your help," Felix said, despite his disappointment.

"No sweat, man," Jim said. "Let me know if you need anything else. Just try what I told you. If she is still sick, give me a call, and I'll walk over."

"Thanks."

"You bet."

Following Jim's advice, Felix boiled a pot of water to make coffee in a French press. As he waited for the water to boil, he began to feel a little better. The mental lapses seemed to have disappeared, though he still felt periodic dizzy spells. He tapped Greta's shoulder, to make sure she was still breathing, then prepared a cup of coffee with milk and sugar for her. She took sips amid low sobs and the continuous plea for him to call 911.

"Just finish the coffee, and then drink some juice and water. You'll be fine," Felix tried to comfort her. "If it doesn't stop, then we'll call nine-one-one, okay? The friend of mine I just spoke to said it's probably just a bad trip and that it will soon go away."

Greta went on to take big sips of the coffee, like a child who had been convinced of the goodness of a drink or medicine and had gulped it down in hopes of an immediate recovery. Felix noticed that Greta's body was still shaking, her skin turning into colors he had never before seen on any person: dark rings beneath her eyes, bluish lines on her chest and neck, and some red spots on her cheeks.

The two drank some orange juice and water and afterward decided to get dressed and go for a walk. They held on to each other's arms, as if their mere closeness guaranteed each other's survival. They made a right on exiting the building and headed toward Prospect Park. The air had thinned out over the course of the night and had turned into a fresh, pleasant breeze. Felix inhaled deeply, hoping it would dilute the odious gas trapped inside his lungs. Greta remained sullen and apprehensive; her eyes darted in all directions as if expecting someone to sneak up on them. The freshness of the breeze didn't seem to have any impact on her mood or physical condition. In fact, her face seemed to sag around her horror-filled eyes. She walked a step behind Felix, her hand locked in his bent elbow.

They stopped at the corner of Fourteenth Street and Eighth Avenue, to wait for an approaching car to pass before they crossed. Though they hadn't seen anyone since they stepped out of the building, Greta suddenly began, "Let's watch our backs, someone is following us."

"Greta, there is no one out here," Felix said, and looked around them to verify his claim.

"I think someone is trying to kill us, we should go back to the apartment and call nine-one-one," she said, and grabbed onto Felix's arm, refusing to let him walk any farther. The car's driver looked at the couple suspiciously from his window as he drove past; he slowed down to a stop a few yards from them. Greta broke into a run, shouting, "He is coming after us." Felix chased after her.

"What are you doing?" he screamed when he caught up with her a few feet away.

"Let's go back to the apartment, please. I am afraid I am going—"

Using his right palm, Felix covered her mouth and said, "Please do me a favor and chill. Just relax, all right? Everything will be fine!"

"Wait a minute," she said, looking intently in his eyes.

"What is it?"

She paused, her eyes trained on his face as if to confirm some suspicion of hers.

"What?" he asked.

"You look like Bill Cosby," she said.

Suddenly the rapid heartbeat, the sharp pain in the head, and the dizziness all came back in full force. Felix felt he was losing his balance and held on to Greta's arm to steady himself. He was cold and feverish, his body shivering. They held each other's arm tightly and hurried back to the apartment, as if they were being pursued by a pack of hounds. I? Look like Bill Cosby? Felix thought. Did she actually say that? She must be completely out of her fucking mind! He turned to face Greta. She looked like a trapped animal. *A loaded white chick gets fucked up on her first date with a black dude?* Jim's words repeated in his head.

She is a rich white chick indeed, Felix thought, but she digs my shit; and what really matters at the end of the day is someone who digs your shit, no matter how funky it is! In contrast to those emotionally high-maintenance and sexually preclusive black women in Park Slope, and their turbaned and dreadlock-adorned counterparts in Fort Greene, white girls are sexually liberated, Felix's mind drifted on. They fuck or marry who they want without any sociological or pathological hang-ups. He pondered why these well-educated black women often would not give the time of the day to smart and intelligent cats like himself or the white boys who chased after them. Instead they settled only for regular black men, who most often turned out to be too black for them. Call it the dilemma of the modern urban black woman, Felix thought, and immediately concocted an idea of writing a book of polemical essays dealing with this issue. He would call it *The Sexual-Erotic and Social Dilemma of the Modern and Urban Black Woman in the Twenty-first Century*. The anthropologists and African studies gurus will eat it up, Felix thought. He was already imagining the success of an essay capable of drawing parallels with W. E. B. DuBois's notion of the "color line" as the main problem to be faced by America in the twentieth century. His *The Sexual-Erotic and Social Dilemma . . .* would make the case that the modern urban black woman's historical renunciation of erotic and emotional relationships with white men (a direct result of the white man's defilement of their womanhood from the time of slavery up to the sixties) would come to an end upon her realization that most of the black men she considered up to par with her beauty, knowledge, and social caliber were being snatched up and married by white women. From the Nobel laureate Wole Soyinka to the United States Supreme Court justice Clarence Thomas; from blues and jazz musicians, painters and photographers, to diplomats, poets and intellectuals—you name them. Felix would argue, "They all marry white women." And he hoped to conclude in *The Sexual-Erotic and Social Dilemma of the Modern and Urban Black Woman in the Twenty-first Century* that those intelligent and gorgeous Nefertiti and Cleopatra look-alikes in Park Slope and Fort Greene would eventually evaluate their loneliness and reckon with the fact that it was high time they rid their hearts of their "sentimental" bias against white men and start dating and marrying Caucasians, just as their female counterparts have been doing for years.

As hazy as his mental condition was, Felix believed, and firmly so, that he was onto something monumental here.

The moment the couple reentered the apartment Greta crashed on the futon. Her face and neck were dotted with red and dark spots. Dark ones had replaced the blue lines on her neck, though a faint trace of the blue remained there. Felix's head began to spin again, and for a brief moment he contemplated calling the emergency room at Park Slope's Methodist Hospital; but recalling Jim's warnings, he decided against it. It seemed to Felix as if a whole day had passed since he had spoken to Jim. He knew he had to do something immediately. Greta's eyes were half-closed, and seemed to be turning inward. He shook her arm. Only a twitch appeared on her face. After a strenuous effort he managed to lift her up, and with her full weight resting on his similarly weak and unstable body, he walked Greta gingerly to the bedroom. As they walked from the living room, Greta's right thigh rubbed against the stereo amplifier, turning the stereo's volume knob up by quite a few notches. Rachmaninov was suddenly as loud and yet as delicate as ever. Felix was not even aware until then that the record was still playing.

Like one on a life-saving mission, Felix hastily undressed Greta on the frameless floor futon bed. He only removed her shoes, skirt, and underwear—a negligible white thong that glowed in the dark. Her long white legs looked even whiter in contrast to the semidarkness of the room, which was illuminated only by a faint light that came from the street. She looked like a sedated patient on an operating table, waiting for the team of doctors and nurses to start burying their surgical knives in her flesh.

Zeus appeared on the windowsill, purring and apparently taking notice of what went on. Felix was somewhat comforted by the cat's presence, ascribing some magical or karmic importance to it.

He unbuckled his belt and removed his pants and underwear. He slowly mounted himself between Greta's outstretched legs, and using his fingers, cleared a path through her dense, wild bush. Felix was surprised by this when they had made love the first time; he had expected Greta to have a clean-shaven or even waxed vaginal area.

A few minutes later Felix managed to penetrate her, though not without scratching the tight skin of his penis, which was painful. He could not tell if Greta was feeling some pain as well; her face was blank, like that of someone enjoying a deep sleep. He continued, nonetheless, and jerked and gyrated in and out of her with a force and determination he had never known before, a determination possessed only by one on a life-saving mission like his.

Some ten or twenty minutes into the ordeal, which in Felix's head ran anywhere between five minutes to an hour, Greta suddenly screamed, "Yes, Cosby! Yes, Cosby!" Zeus jumped from the windowsill and bolted from the room, meowing. Felix moaned silently, though he was happy that Greta had at least shown a sign of revival. A few more minutes of intense fucking and she will be fully awake, he thought, and smiled gallantly to himself. He went back to work, exerting even more force from his waist, and carelessly poking his penis in and out of her like the rod of a builder's concrete vibrator, not caring much about its physical impact or where it landed in the matrix. Greta's cries of "Yes, Cosby! Fuck me, Cosby. Fuck me!" got even louder. Fresh sweat beads formed on her forehead, which to Felix was another good sign, indicating the rise in her body temperature and heartbeat. He rammed even harder and moments later became completely lost in the rhythm of his own vibration, reaching a whole new altitude of chemical and mental fusion. The substance they had smoked seemed to be having its final effect on Felix at that moment. He felt a massive explosion in his head and through his body. Greta broke from the rhythm of her litany of "Yes, Cosby, yes!" and out of the blue asked her lover, "Is that you, Felix? You look like Bill Cosby."

Felix picked up the pace, penetrating her even deeper and harder, putting his entire torso into each descent. A few moments later, Greta cried out loudly, "Felix, Cosby, Felix, Cosby," in an exultant, yet painful, voice. But Felix's faculties, along with his mind and part of his soul, had already deserted his body; each acted on its own volition and all reacted simultaneously as if in a sudden combustion.

And long after he had stopped hearing Greta's voice and her moanings and agonizing cries, Felix's body maintained the rhythm of his up-and-down motions to the accompaniment of Rachmaninov's piano.

MALLAM SILE

Nothing is harder than to accept oneself. Actually only the naive succeed in doing it, and I have so far met very few people in my world who could be described as naive in this positive sense.

MAX FRISCH, *I'M NOT STILLER*

1.

He was popularly known as *mai tea*, or the tea seller. His shop was located right in the navel of Zongo Street—a stone's throw from the chief's assembly shed and adjacent to the kiosk where Mansa BBC, the town gossip, sold her provisions. Along with fried eggs and white butter bread, Mallam Sile carried all kinds of beverages: regular black tea, Japanese green tea, milo, *bournvita*, cocoa drink, instant coffee. But on Zongo Street all hot beverages were referred to as just tea, and it was usual, therefore, to hear people say, "Mallam Sile, may I have a mug of cocoa tea?" or "Silo, may I have a cup of coffee tea?"

The tea shop had no windows. It was built of *wawa*, a cheap wood easily infested by termites. The floor was uncemented, and heaps of dust rose in the air anytime a customer walked in. Sile protected his merchandise from the dust by keeping everything in plastic bags. An enormous wooden "chop box," the top of which he used as serving table, covered most of the space in the shop. There was a tall chair behind the chop box for Sile, but he never used it, preferring instead to stand on his feet even when the shop was empty. There were also three benches that were meant to be used only by those who bought tea from Sile, though the idle gossips who crowded the shop occupied the seats most of the time.

Old Sile had an irrational fear of being electrocuted, and so, never tapped electricity into his shack, as was usually done on Zongo Street. Instead, he used kerosene lanterns, three of which hung from the low wooden ceiling. Sile kept a small radio in the shop, and whenever he had no customers, he listened, in meditative silence, to the English programs on GBC 2, as though he understood what was being said. Mallam Sile only spoke his northern Sisala tongue, and knew just enough broken Hausa— the language of the street's inhabitants—to be able to conduct his tea business.

The mornings were usually slow for the tea seller, as a majority of the streetfolks preferred the traditional breakfast of *kókó da mása*, or corn porridge with rice cake. But come evening the shop was crowded with the street's young men and women, who gossiped and talked about the laytes' neus in town. Some, however, went to the shop just to meet their loved ones. During the shop's peak hours—from eight in the evening till around midnight— one could hardly hear himself talk because of the boisterous chattering that went on. But anytime Mallam Sile opened his mouth to add to a conversation, people would say to him, "Shut up, Sile, what do you know about this?" or "Close your beak, Sile, who told you that?" The tea seller learned to swallow his words, and eventually spoke only when he was engaged in a transaction with a customer. But nothing said or even whispered in the shop escaped Sile's quick ears.

Mallam Sile was a loner, without kin on the street or anywhere else in the city. He was born in Nanpugu, a small border town in the north. He left home at age sixteen, and all by himself, journeyed more than nine hundred miles in a cow truck to find work down south in Kumasi—the gold-rich capital city of Ghana's Ashanti region.

Within a week of his arrival in the city Sile landed a houseservant job. And even though his monthly wages were meagre, he still sent a portion of it back home to his poor, ailing parents, who lived like destitutes in their drought-stricken village. But Sile's efforts were not enough to save his parents from the claws of Death, who took them away in their sleep one night. They were found tightly clinging to each other, as if one of them had realized that he or she was about to die and had grabbed the other so they could go together.

The young Sile received the death news with mixed emotions of sadness and joy. He saw it as a deserved rest for his parents, seeing as they were ill and bedridden for many months. Then he made the unusual decision not to attend their funeral, though he sent money for their decent burial. With his parents deceased, Sile suddenly found himself with more money than he usually had. He quit his house-servant job and found another selling iced *kenkey* in Kumasi's central market. Sile kept every pesewa he earned, and two years later he was able to use his savings to open a tea business. It was the first of such establishments on Zongo Street and remained the only one for many years to come.

Mallam Sile was short. In fact, so short that many claimed he was a pygmy. He stood exactly five feet and one inch tall. Although he didn't have the broad flat nose, poorly developed chin, and round head of the pygmies, he was stout and hairy all over—probably his only resemblance to them. A childhood sickness that deteriorated Sile's vision had continued to plague him throughout his adult life. Yet he refused to go to the hospital and condemned any form of medication—tradional or Western. "God is the one who brings illness, and He is the only true healer." That was Sile's simple, if rather mystical, explanation. He believed that the human body in which a disease resides will one day give in to Death, "no matter how long it takes her to catch up with you."

Sile's small face was covered with a thick, long beard. The wrinkles on his dark face and the moistness of his soft squinted eyes gave him the appearance of a sage, one who had lived through and conquered many adversities in his life. His smile, which stretched from one wrinkled cheek to the other, baring his kola-stained teeth, attested to his strength, wisdom, and self-confidence.

Sile wore the same outfit every day: a white polyester jalabia and its matching *wando*, a loose pair of slacks that used strings at the waist. He had eight of these suits, and wore a different one each day of the week. Also, Sile's perpetually shaven head was never seen without his white embroidered Mecca hat—worn by highly devout Muslims as a reflection of their submission to Allah. Like most of the street's dwellers, Sile had only one pair of slippers at a time, and replaced them only after they were worn out beyond any feasible repair. An unusual birth defect that caused the tea seller to grow an additional toe on each foot made it impossible for him to find footwear that fit him properly; special slippers were made for him by Anába the cobbler, who used discarded car tires for the soles of the shoes he made. The rascals, led by Samadu, the street's most notorious bully, poked at Sile's feet and his slippers, which they called *kalabilwala*, a nonsensical term no one could understand, let alone translate.

2.

At forty-six Mallam Sile was still a virgin. He routinely made passes at the divorcées and widows who came to his shop, but none showed any interest in him whatsoever. "What is one going to do with a dwarf?" the women would ask, feeling ashamed of having passes made at them by Sile. A couple of them, however, were receptive to Sile's advances, though everyone knew the girls flirted with him so they could get free tea.

Eventually, Sile resigned himself to his lack of success with women and was even convinced he would die a virgin. Yet late at night, after all the customers, gossips, idlers, and rumormongers had left the shop to seek refuge in their shanties and on their bug-ridden grass mattresses, Sile would be heard singing love songs, hoping that a woman somewhere would respond to his passionate cries.

A beautiful woman, they say,
Is like an elephant's meat.
And only the man with the sharpest knife
Can cut through.
That's what they say.

Young girl, I have no knife,
I am not a hunter of meat,
And I am not savage.
I am only looking for love.
This is what I say.

Up North where I am from,
Young girls are not what they are here.
Up North where I am from,
People don't judge you by your knife.
They look at the size of your heart.

Young girl, I don't know what you look like.
I don't know where to look for you.
I don't even know who you are, young girl.
All I know is: my heart is aching.

Oh, Oh, Oh! My heart is aching for you.

Sile's voice rang with melancholy when he sang his songs. But still, the rascals derided him. "When at all are you going to give up, Sile?" they would say. "Can't you see that no woman would marry you?"

"I have given up on them long, long ago," he would reply, "but I am never going to give up on myself!"

"You keep fooling yourself," they would tell him, laughing.

The rascals' mocking of Sile didn't end just there. Knowing he didn't see properly, they used fake or banned cedi notes to purchase tea from Mallam Sile at night. The tea seller pinned the useless currency notes on the wall as if they were good-luck charms. He believed that it was hunger—and not mischief—that had led the rascals to cheat him. And since Mallam Sile considered it "inhuman to refuse a hungry person food," he allowed them to get away with their frauds.

When Sile cooled off hot tea for customers, he poured the contents of one mug into another, raising one over the other. The rascals would push Sile's arms in the middle of this process, causing the hot beverage to spill all over his arms. The tea seller was never angered by such pranks. He merely grinned and flashed his cola-stained teeth, and without saying a word, wiped off the spilt tea and continued to serve his customers.

The rascals did even worse things to the poor tea seller. They blew out the lanterns in the shop, so as to steal bread and milo while he tried to rekindle the light. He forgave that and many other pranks as they occurred, effectively ridding his heart of any ill feelings. He waved his short arms to anyone who walked passed his shop front. "How are the Heavens with you, boy?" he would shout in greeting. Sile called everyone "boy," including women and older people, and he hardly said a sentence without referring to the Heavens.

He prided himself on his hard work, and smiled anytime he looked in the mirror and saw his dwarfish appearance and ailing eyes, two abnormalities he had grown to accept with an inner joy no one could understand. A few months before the death of his parents, he had come to the conclusion that if Allah had created him any different than how he was, he wouldn't have been Mallam Sile—an individual Sile's heart, soul, and spirit had grown to accept and respect. This created an inner peace within him that made it possible for him not only to tolerate the ill treatment meted out to him by the street's rascals, but to also forgive them of their actions. Though in their eyes, Sile was only a buffoon.

3.

One sunny afternoon during the dry season, Mallam Sile was seen atop the roof of his shack with hammers, saws, pincers, and all kinds of building tools. He tarried there all day long like a lizard, and by dusk he had dismantled all the aluminum roofing sheets that had once sheltered him and his business. He resumed work early the following morning, and around one-thirty before *azafar*, the first of the two afternoon prayers, Sile had no place to call either home or tea shop—he had demolished the shack down to its dusty floor.

At three-thirty after *la-asar*, the second afternoon worship, Mallam Sile moved his personal belongings and all his tea paraphernalia to a room in the servants' quarters of the chief's palace. The room was arranged for him by the chief's *wazeer*, or right-hand man, who was sympathetic to the tea seller.

During the next two days, Mallam Sile ordered plywood and

odum boards, a wood superior to the *wawa* used for the old shop. He also ordered a few bags of cement and truckloads of sand and stones, and immediately began building a new shack— a much bigger one this time.

The streetfolks were shocked by Sile's new building and wondered where he got the money to embark on such a big enterprise. Sile was rumored to be constructing a minimarket store to rub shoulders with Alhaji Saifa, the owner of the street's provision store. And even though the tea seller categorically denied the rumor, it rapidly gained ground on the street, eventually creating bad blood between Sile and Alhaji Saifa.

It took three days for Mallam Sile to complete work on the new shop's foundation, and it took an additional three weeks for him to erect the wooden walls and the aluminum roofing sheets. While Sile was busy at work, passersby would call out, "How is the provision store coming?" or "Mai-tea, how is the mansion coming?" Sile would reply simply: "It is coming well, boy. It will be completed soon, *Insha Allah*." He would grin his usual wide grin and wave his short hairy arms, and then return to his work.

Meanwhile, as the days and weeks passed, the streetfolks grew impatient and somewhat angry at the closing of Sile's shop. The nearest tea shack was three hundred meters away, on Zerikyi Road—and not only that; the owner of the shack, Abongo, was generally abhorred by the streetfolks. And it was for a good reason. Abongo, also a northerner, was quite unfriendly even to his loyal customers. He maintained a rigid NO CREDIT policy at his shop, and had customers pay him before they were even served. No one was an exception to this policy—even if he or she were dying of hunger. And unlike Sile, Abongo didn't tolerate idlers or loud conversation in his shop. If a customer persisted in chatting, Abongo reached for his mug, poured the content in a plastic basin, and refunded his money to him. He then chased the customer out of the shop, brandishing his bullwhip and cursing after him, "If your mama and papa never teach you manners, I'll teach you some. I'll sew those careless lips of yours together, you bastard son of a bastard woman!"

It wasn't for another three weeks that Mallam Sile's shop was finally reopened. Immediately after work on the shop was completed Sile left for his hometown. He returned one Friday evening, flanked by a stern, fat woman who looked to be in her late thirties and was three times larger than the tea seller. The woman, whose name was Abeeba, turned out to be Mallam Sile's wife. Abeeba was tall and massive, with a face as gloomy as that of someone mourning a dead relative. Just like her husband, Abeeba said very little to people in and out of the shop. She, too, grinned and waved her huge arms anytime she greeted people, though unlike the tea seller, malice seemed to lurk behind Abeeba's cheerful smile. She carried herself with the grace and confidence of a lioness, and covered her head and parts of her face in an Islamic veil, a practice being dropped by most married women on Zongo Street.

The rascals asked Sile when they ran into him at the market, "From where did you get this elephant? Better not be on her bad side; she'll sit on you till you sink into the ground." To this, the tea seller did not say a word, knowing his response would only incite more cynical pronouncements.

4.

Exactly one week after Sile's return from his village, he and his wife opened the doors of their new shop to their customers. Among the most talked-about features of the new shop on opening night was the smooth concrete floor and the bright gas lantern that illuminated every corner of the shop. The streetfolks were equally impressed by the whitewashed odum boards used for the walls, quite a departure from the termite-infested *wawa* boards of the old shop. And in a small wooden box behind the counter, Sile and his wife burned *tularen mayu*, or witches' lavender, a strong yet sweet-smelling incense that doubled as a jinx repellent— to drive away bad spirits from the establishment.

On the first night the tea shop was so crowded that some customers couldn't even find a seat on the twelve new folding metal chairs Sile had bought. The patrons sang songs of praise to the variety of food on the new menu, which included meat pie, brown bread, custard, and "tom brown," an imported grain porridge. Some of the patrons even went as far as thanking Sile and his wife for relieving them of "Abongo's nastiness." But wise old Sile, who was as familiar with the streetfolks' cynicism as he was with the palms of his hands, merely nodded and grinned his sheepish, innocent grin. He knew that despite the praises they heaped on him, and the numerous smiles being flashed his way, some customers were at that very moment thinking of ways to cheat him. Though unbeknown to both Sile and his future predators, those days of cheating and prank-playing would soon be gone, forever. And it wasn't that Mallam Sile had suddenly metamorphosed into a mean fellow or anything of that sort. It was, instead, because of Abeeba, whose serious, daunting face and gigantic presence scared off those who came to the shop with the intention of cheating the tea seller.

While Sile prepared the tea and other foods on the menu, Abeeba served and collected the money. She tried to convince her husband that they, too, should adopt Abongo's NO CREDIT policy. Sile had quickly frowned upon the idea, claiming that it was inhumane to do such a thing. Abeeba had pointed out to Sile that most of those who asked for credit and ended up stiffing him were not "poor and hungry folks," as Sile expressed it, but cheats who continued to take advantage of his leniency.

Mallam Sile and his wife debated the matter for three days before they came to a compromise. They agreed to extend credit, but only in special cases and also on the condition that the debtor swore by the Koran to pay on time; and that if a debtor didn't make a payment, he or she would not be given any credit in the future. But hardly had the tea seller and his wife resumed extending credit to these patrons when some of them resorted to the old habit of skipping their payments. However, an encounter between Abeeba and one of the defaulters helped change everything, including the way Sile was treated on the street. And what took place was this.

•   •   •

Like most of the city's neighborhoods, Zongo Street had its own "tough guy," a young man considered the strongest among his peers. Samadu, a pugnacious sixteen-year-old bully whose fame had reached every corner of the city, was Zongo Street's tough guy. He was of a median height, muscular, and a natural-born athlete. And for nine months running, no kid or neighborhood bully had managed to put Samadu's back to the ground in the haphazard wrestling contests held beside the central market's latrine. Samadu's "power" was such that parents paid him to protect their children from other bullies at school. He was also known for torturing and even killing the livestock of the adults who denounced him. If they didn't have pets or domestic animals, he harassed their children for several days, until he was appeased in cash or goods. Some parents won Samadu's friendship for their children by bribing him with occasional gifts of money, food, or clothing.

One could therefore imagine the stir it caused when on an early Tuesday morning Mallam Sile's wife showed up at Samadu's house to collect a tea debt he owed them. Prior to that, Abeeba had tried amicably to collect the money Samadu owed them, which was eighty cedis—about four dollars. After her third futile attempt, Abeeba suggested to Sile that they use force to retrieve the money. But Sile had quickly cautioned his wife, "Stay out of that boy's way, he is dangerous. And if he has decided not to pay, please let him keep the amount. He will be the loser in the end."

"But, Mallam, it is an insult what he is doing," Abeeba had argued. "I think people to whom we have been generous should only be generous in return. I am getting fed up with their ways, and the sooner the folks here know that even the toad gets sick of filling his belly with the same dirty pond water every day, the better!" Sile begged his wife to let the matter die, but all she said to him was, "I will, once I set a few things straight around here." Though Sile wasn't sure what his wife meant by that, he did not say a word afterward.

When Abeeba arrived at Samadu's house, a number of housewives and young women were busily doing their morning chores in and around the compound—some sweeping and stirring up dust, others fetching water from the tap in the center of the compound and pouring it into the barrels in front of their rooms, and a few were lighting up charcoal pots to warm up hot water and leftovers from the previous night. Abeeba greeted the women politely and asked to be shown to the tough guy's door. The women were hesitant to show her Samadu's room, as Abeeba refused to disclose what had brought her to see the tough guy. Seeing the fire in her eyes, the housewives reluctantly directed her to Samadu's room, located outside the main compound.

The usual tactic the street's teenage boys used when fighting girls or women was to try and strip them of the wrapper around their waist, knowing that they would be unwilling to keep fighting half-naked. Abeeba had therefore worn a sleeveless ready-to-fight shirt and a pair of tight-fitting khaki shorts, and for the first time ever, left her veil at home.

"You rogue, if you call yourself a *man*, come out and pay your debt," Abeeba shouted, and pounded her fist at Samadu's door.

"Who do you think you are? Ruining my sleep because of

some useless eighty cedis?" screamed Samadu from behind the door.

"The money may be useless, but it is certainly worthier than you, and that's why you haven't been able to pay," Abeeba responded. "You rubbish heap of a *man*!" Her voice was coarse and full of menace. The veins on her neck stood erect, like those juju (voodoo) fighters at the annual wrestling contest. Her eyes looked hard and brutish, and she moved her head in rapid movements as if she were having a fit of some sort.

One of the onlookers, a famished-looking housewife, pleaded with the tea seller's wife, "Go back to your house, woman. Don't fight *him*, he would disgrace you in public." Another woman added in the background, "What kind of a woman thinks she can fight a a *man*? Be careful, O!" Abeeba didn't pay any attention to the women's admonitions, which she considered useless babble. Samadu, meanwhile, hadn't yet come out.

Abeeba grabbed the door knob and tried to force it open. A loud bang was heard from the room. She retreated and waited for Samadu to emerge.

A few seconds later the door swung open, and Samadu stormed out, his face clearly showing the anger and red malice that was in his heart. "No one gets away with insulting me. No one!" he screamed. His right cheek was smeared with dried drool, and a whitish mucus gathered at the ends of his eyes. "You ugly elephant-woman. After I am done with you today, you'll learn a lesson or two about why women don't grow beards!" he shouted.

"Haa, you teach me a lesson? You?" screamed Abeeba. "I will educate *you*, about the need to have money in your pocket before you flag the candy man!" She immediately lunged at Samadu.

The women placed their palms on their breasts, shaking their bodies in dread of what was about to happen. "Where are the men on the street? Come and separate the fight, O! Men, come out, O!" they shouted. The children in the compound, though freshly aroused from sleep, jumped excitedly as if watching a ritual. Half of them called out, "*Piri pirin pi,*" while the other half responded, "*Wein son!*" as they chanted and cheered for Samadu.

Samadu knew immediately that if he engaged Abeeba in a wrestling match, she would use her bulky mass to force him to the ground. His strategy, therefore, was to throw punches and kicks from a safe distance, thereby avoiding direct contact with her. But soon after the fight erupted he realized that Abeeba was a lot quicker than he had presumed, since she managed to dodge the first five punches he had thrown at her. He threw a sixth punch, and missed. He stumbled on his own foot when he tried to connect the seventh blow, and he landed within a foot of Abeeba. With a blinding quickness she seized Samadu by the sleeping wrapper tied around his neck and began to punch him. The crowd's exuberance was dimmed by this unexpected turn of events. No sound was heard anywhere as Abeeba continued her attack on the tough guy.

But Samadu wasn't heralded as the street's tough guy for nothing. He threw a sharp jab at Abeeba's stomach and somehow managed to release himself from her grip by deftly undoing the knot of his sleeping cloth. He was topless now, and clad only in a pair of corduroy knickers. He danced his feet, swung his arms, and moved his chest sideways, like true boxers did. The crowd got excited again. "*Piri pirin pi, Wein son! Piri pirin pi, Wein son!*" they sang. Some among them shouted "Ali, Ali, Ali!" as Samadu danced and pranced, carefully avoiding Abeeba, who watched his movements with the keenness of a hungry lioness, hoping for a slip so she could tackle him.

The women in the crowd went from holding their breasts to slapping their massive thighs. They jumped about nervously, their bodies moving in rhythm to the chants. The boys booed Abeeba, calling her all sorts of names that equated her with the beasts of the jungle. "Destroy that elephant," they screamed.

The harder the crowd cheered for Samadu, the fancier his footwork became. He finally threw a punch that landed on Abeeba's left shoulder, though she seemed completely unfazed by the blow, as she continued to chase him around the small circle created by the spectators. With all the might he could muster Samadu threw another fist, but Abeeba had already anticipated it. She dodged, then deftly grabbed Samadu's wrist and twisted his arm with such force that he let out a high-pitched cry, "*Wayyo!*" The crowd gasped and watched nervously as the tough guy attempted to extricate himself from Abeeba's tight grip. He tightened all the muscles in his body and moved his head from side to side—all in an attempt to foil Abeeba's move. But her strength was just too much for him.

The crowd booed, "*Wooh*, ugly rhinoceros." Then, in a sudden, swift movement, Abeeba hurled the tough guy off the ground, then lifted him farther up above her head (the crowd booed louder), before dumping him on the ground, like a sack of rice. She jumped quickly on top of him and began to whack him violently.

The women jumped about frantically, like scared antelopes. They shouted, "Where are the men in this house?" Men, come out, O! There is a fight!"

A few men came running to the scene, followed by many more a few minutes later.

Meanwhile Abeeba continued her offensive. With each punch that landed on Samadu, she asked, "Where is our money?"

"I don't have it, and wouldn't pay even if I had it!" Samadu responded in an attempt to regain his shattered pride and dignity. The men drew nearer and attempted to pull Abeeba away from her victim, but that turned out to be a difficult task; her grip on Samadu's waistband was too firm. The men pleaded on Samadu's behalf and begged Abeeba to let go of her captive. "I'll not release him until he pays us back our money," she shouted. "And if he doesn't I'll drag his ass all the way to the Zongo police station," she added.

On hearing this, an elderly man who lived in Samadu's compound ran inside the house; he returned a few minutes later with eighty cedis, which he placed in the palm of Abeeba's free hand. With one hand gripping Samadu's waistband, she used the fingers of the other to flip and count the money. She released him once she was sure the amount added up to the eighty cedis Samadu owed her and husband. She gave the tough guy a mean, hard look as she left. The awestruck crowd watched silently as

Abeeba walked back to her shack, their mouths agape as if what they had just witnessed was from a cinema reel.

5.

Mallam Sile was still engaged in his morning *zikhr*, or meditation, when Abeeba returned to the shack, and of course had no inkling of what had taken place. An hour later, when they were preparing to open the tea shop for their customers, Abeeba announced to Sile that Samadu had paid the money he owed them. The tea seller, though surprised at what he heard, didn't see the need to ask how this had come to pass. In his naiveté, he concluded that perhaps Samadu had paid the debt because he had either found himself a vocation or had finally been "entered by the love and fear of God." Abeeba's announcement confirmed Mallam Sile's long-standing belief that "every man is capable of goodness just as he is capable of evil," and that it is only with time and acquired wisdom that people like Samadu would change their bad ways and become good people.

The tea seller's belief was further solidified when he ran into Samadu a fortnight later. The tough guy greeted him politely, something Samadu had never done before. When Mallam Sile told his wife about the unusual encounter with Samadu, she fought hard to restrain herself from telling him what had actually caused the change in Samadu's attitude. Abeeba also knew that Sile would be quite displeased if he found out the method she had used to retrieve the money. Just a week ago, he had spoken to her about "the uselessness of using fire to put out fire," of how it "worsens rather than extinguishes the original flame." Abeeba only prayed that one of these days someone didn't tell her husband about her duel with Samadu—the entire city seemed to know about it by now. Tough guys from other neighborhoods even came to the tea shop just to steal a glance at the woman who conquered the tough guy of Zongo Street.

Then one night during the fasting month of Ramadan, some two months after the fight, a voice in Mallam Sile's head asked: Why is everyone calling my wife the "man checker"? How come people I give credit suddenly pay me on time? Why am I being treated with such respect, even by the worst and most stubborn rascals on the street? Mallam Sile was lying in bed with his wife at the time these questions popped in his head. In his usual fashion, he didn't think any further of the questions or even try to answer them. He drew in a deep breath and began to pray in his heart. He smiled and thanked Allahu-Raheemu, the Merciful One, for curing the streetfolks of the prejudice they had nursed against him for so long. Mallam Sile also thanked Allah for giving his neighbors the will and the courage to finally accept him just as he was created. He flashed a grin in the darkness and moved closer to his slumbering wife. He buried his small body in her massive, protective frame and soon fell into a deep, dreamless sleep.

FAITH

At about six o'clock on the morning of August 13, Suf-yan heard a loud siren outside his bedroom window. Accustomed to the incessant noises of the city's car alarms and garbage truck engines, his natural instinct was to go back to sleep. He pulled the bedsheet from below his waist and covered his whole body, leaving only his head to stick out. He closed his eyes amid the loudness and growing intensity of the siren, and soon after drifted back to sleep.

But shortly, the ground beneath his building began to shake vigorously. Objects flew and crashed into each other in the one-bedroom apartment he shared with his wife, Pas-cal. Within seconds the apartment floor caved in, and then the entire building easily came crumbling down. Suf-yan fell through the six floors of the building, though miraculously his body didn't hit anything during the descent.

As quickly as the building had collapsed, the dust of the crash settled, exposing an expanse of desertlike land that went on for miles with nothing in sight. The apartment buildings and the brownstones lining Washington Avenue in Suf-yan's Fort Greene neighborhood, the side trees, the parked cars, the subway entrance signposts at Washington and Lafayette Street, all seemed to have evaporated into nothingness.

He panicked.

Where is Pas-cal? Where is Pas-cal?

There was dead silence.

"Pas-cal, Pas-cal, where are you?" he screamed.

All he could hear was the distant echo of his voice.

He turned and looked all around him, in the hope of locating the tower clock in the heart of downtown Brooklyn he used to tell time and as a point of navigational reference. But the landmarked edifice had also disappeared.

The next thing Suf-yan knew, thousands of naked men, women, and children began appearing out of nowhere. He looked down at his waist and realized that he, too, was naked—though he had gone to sleep in a white T-shirt and pajama pants. With solemn faces, people stood side by side, as if in readiness for a great expedition. As someone who was very conscious of his body, and to an extent even ashamed of it—because of his stick legs—Suf-yan was surprised that he didn't care at all that his body was exposed. Everyone, it seemed, was more preoccupied with the unusual circumstances they had found themselves in than with worrying about their nakedness.

Suf-yan recognized a handful of faces among the crowd. There was one person representing every stage of his life: Muhsin, his childhood friend, who was killed during a soccer stadium stampede when they were twelve. There were also Mina, his first crush, and Blake, his best friend and business partner in their small architectural firm. Ron-E, Suf-yan's painter friend who lived in Williamsburg, was also present, and so was Ram-lah, Suf-yan's ex-wife.

"But how did she get here?" Suf-yan wondered of Ram-lah, a staunch Muslim woman he had married from his Ghanaian hometown. She had divorced Suf-yan after only three years of marriage, citing his "lack of seriousness with the religion." She then married another Ghanaian, a more committed Muslim, and had moved to live with him in Atlanta, Georgia. Suf-yan considered himself lucky that he and Ram-lah didn't have any children before their separation.

Of all the familiar faces around him, the one whose presence intrigued Suf-yan the most was Liya's. Liya was Suf-yan's older sister, his mother's first child. But he had never seen his sister before. She had died when she was only three months old, some four years before Suf-yan's own birth. Yet, Suf-yan had no doubt that the girl who stood only a few meters away was his dear sister. She stared at him for a few moments and then zigzagged her way through the crowd to join a separate group that was just forming to the right of the mass of the adults. Like everyone in her group, Liya looked to be in her early teens; and also, every boy and girl in the group was about the same height—five feet tall or so—and bore the same physical features: muscular with lots of beautiful curly dark hair. They wore bright, confident, and precocious smiles, not at all the same worried look the adults all wore.

Suf-yan wanted to call to his sister, but his voice was muted. Suf-yan longed for his wife or someone to shout, "Wake up, Suf-yan. You were only having a nightmare!" He imagined how relieved he would have been if everything that was happening was just a dream. With the exception of the teenagers, everyone around Suf-yan looked pensive, with eyes staring into the distance and eyebrows knitted in a furrow.

The sky seemed like a low flat ceiling that stretched for thousands of miles; it was so low that Suf-yan felt he could lift up his hand and touch it. The sun was also close, dipping lower and lower toward the earth, its rays scorching the skins of the people in the crowd. Like a flock of migratory birds, compelled by symbiotic awareness of their landscape and advised by instinct, the crowd began a fast-paced march forward. Though unlike birds, the marchers had no destination in mind.

Every few steps, Suf-yan found himself flanked by different people. In one instance it would be two black women, and the next moment a white man and a Chinese woman. At one point he even found himself walking alongside his ex-wife, his parents, and his favorite college professor, Mr. Alfred Johannsen, whose "Western Thought" class prompted Suf-yan to seriously question the concept of religion. It was a game of human chess, people strategically switching places.

It then occurred to Suf-yan that he was witnessing exactly what Ustaz Hashim, his childhood madrassa teacher, had claimed would happen on *Alyau mul Quiyam*, or the Day of Judgment. "On the Day of Judgment, seven thousand angels, acting on direct orders from Allah, will raze down the universe, with all its material and natural contents, and fold it up like a mat," Ustaz Hashim had once told Suf-yan's class. He had then depicted in graphic details how "Allah will lower the sun closer to earth until it cooks the brains in our heads. It is Allahu Ta-ala's way of letting us know that for our entire existence he has been holding the sun and the sea at bay, so they don't destroy us. But on this day Allah will let loose all the elements before he commands his angels to fold the earth like one folds a mat. He will then raise all of us from our graves, and every human being will be naked, the same way we came into the world!"

Even as a twelve year old, Suf-yan had developed plenty of doubts about the Day of Judgment, something he thought of as a hoax, an attempt by humans to give meaning to life's chaos and misery—to make life worth living.

Once during the question-and-answer session that followed his teacher's gloom and doom lecture, Suf-yan raised up his right hand and asked, "Is Allah going to wait for everyone to die before *Alyau mul Quiyam* starts?" Though the question took him by surprise, Ustaz Hashim made a desperate attempt to answer it. "Maybe not every human being would be dead by the day Allah decides to hold court," he told the class. "But know that Allah does what He wants and at any time He wishes to, and therefore only He alone knows what is going to happen *tomorrow*."

During Wednesday's Bible study, the pastor at Suf-yan's parochial elementary school also insisted that "The signs of Judgment Day are everywhere. Women in men's clothes, greediness, the rampant adultery and fornication by men, women, and young children, women bleaching their skins and perming their hair, and so many other signs I can't even mention. In fact, the day is upon us!" But neither the certainty of his teacher's frightening account of the Day of Judgment nor the pastor's disturbing warnings were enough to prevent the growing doubts in Suf-yan's mind about how the world was going to end. Something about the metaphysical and magical nature of all he had heard sounded too good to be true to him.

Though both teachers may have gotten a detail or two wrong in their separate accounts of how the day would unfold, their prediction turned out to be as real as could be. And with this reality came the painful realization to Suf-yan that, soon, he would be one of the millions or even billions that would be sent to Hell, where their bodies would be "used as fuel for Hell's everlasting fire," as Ustaz Hashim once told them. "A person who doesn't believe in the Day of Judgment was just as condemned to Hell as someone who doesn't believe in the first and most important principle of Islam, *Laailaa ha illallah!*" [There is no entity worthy of worship but Allah!]

As the great march continued, millions more people joined. Some rose from the ground, spewed by the earth that had swallowed them for eons. Others simply appeared out of nowhere, and Suf-yan figured that those may be the humans whose bodies were cremated after their deaths.

After marching for what felt like an eternity, the multitude suddenly encountered a gigantic building in front of them. Though the building was still hundreds of miles away, Suf-yan could still tell it was the Empire State Building. Thousands of white and black angels and jinns flew in and around the building, as they feverishly prepared for the day's activities. According to Suf-yan's madrassa teacher, the actual judgment proceedings, which would take tens of years in real time, would be condensed to a mere six hours, from sunrise to noon.

All four sides of the Empire State Building were draped by

black and white flags. The last three levels of the building—
which turned into a lighting wonder at night—were drowned in
three different shades of silver, with the lightest at the bottom.
Suf-yan recalled that last January, all three levels were lighted
green, to celebrate the seventy-fifth anniversary of Popeye the
Sailor, the spinach-eating cartoon character. At the highest point
of the building, where the radio and satellite antennas once were,
sat a large, radiant, perfectly rounded globe.

Then, just as the crowd had begun marching without any
provocation, they came to a stop. Like concertgoers waiting for
the star of the show to descend from the sky, everyone just stood
around and stared at the globe. The scene reminded Suf-yan of
pictures he had seen of pilgrims marching to the Quaba, the
"Black Dome of Mecca": millions of worshippers gathered there
each year, to touch the dome's holy walls, so as to receive eternal
blessing and *Aljannah*, Heaven. The big difference here was the
number of people present—billions, the entire human race.

As the sun continued its assault on people's naked bodies,
someone started crying. Soon many more were crying and
screaming for help from the prophets of the religions to which
they belonged, while splintering into different groups based on
those religions. Suf-yan joined the Muslims, who cried, "Save us,
Muhammad, save us!" The Christians called out the name of
Jesus, the Buddhists shouted, "Gautama." There were names of
prophets like Ofosigye, of an African religion, and Ditrampas,
the goddess of a religion from India. But one by one, all the
prophets and messengers of Allah or God or whatever anyone
called their God—from Moses to Muhammad—announced to

their followers that they should plead directly to the "One Above," the Beneficent, the Merciful, as He was the only entity with the power to save anyone on this day.

Soon after the prophets made their announcements, a siren—much like the one that had first awakened Suf-yan—was heard, followed by sparks of lights that came from the globe atop the Empire State Building. The sparks seemed to emanate from a boiling matter within the globe, and they flew hundreds of miles in every direction, touching every single person in the crowd, and in effect, returning the people's skins to normal, soothing the burns they had suffered from the sun. Then, just as Suf-yan's teacher had described, the archangel appeared. He stood to the right of the globe and announced that everyone should start thinking of all they had done on earth—from their very first to their very last minute. The archangel held a Palm Pilot in his left hand, and in a single stroke, using an inkless pen, brought up a minute-by-minute and definitive account of an individual's life.

Here, Suf-yan couldn't help making a mental note of the error in his teacher's account about the archangel's database device. His teacher had narrated that the archangel would be holding a long tablet similar to the one on which Moses had written his ten commandments. Apparently his teacher had seen *The Ten Commandments*, the 1950s epic movie about Moses.

The details of Suf-yan's life began to unravel, flashing into his mind. His abandoning Islam and converting to Buddhism, his use of alcohol, his refusal to pay Zakat (the annual rite of giving a percentage of one's income to the poor), his refusal to perform the Hajj (the pilgrimage to Mecca), and his eating of pork, all things that carried Hell sentences, according to the Koran.

Another loud siren was heard, and then the archangel announced, "Allah has granted a general amnesty to everyone in that group." The archangel pointed at Liya's group, adding that, "They died before their innocence was corrupted, and therefore Allah holds them not liable for any wrong acts they have committed."

A euphoric noise was heard from the group.

"Their books have hereby been closed," added the angel. "And we ask all of them to go straight to Sayed Ibrahim's preparatory school on the east wing of Heaven, and after three years of education they will all be sent to Heaven proper." As the archangel finished, the entire group, numbering in the tens of millions, were whisked away to paradise.

The blanket amnesty given to the children somehow restored hope in Suf-yan that perhaps all was not lost, that perhaps he, too, could be pardoned. And as he waited for his fate, he wondered what had happened to Pas-cal, whom he considered his soulmate. He had not seen her since the previous night, when they went to sleep in the same bed.

Suf-yan's marriage to Ram-lah was arranged in order to satisfy the wish of his mother. But inwardly, he had never believed in having children, his excuse being that at near-forty, he still hadn't mastered his own life and therefore wouldn't want to bring a child into the world.

In Pas-cal, who was a painter, Suf-yan had found the perfect partner, one who not only didn't believe in having children but also denounced marriage entirely. Suf-yan's and Pas-cal's union was one of harmony, love, and respect, and unlike his marriage, involved no other party but the two of them.

But Suf-yan forgot about Pas-cal as quickly as she had come into his mind. Like everyone else on that day, he was concerned about the salvation of only one person: Suf-yan. "On that day not even your children, your mother, your father, or your wife will matter to you; each and every one for himself, Allah for us all," Suf-yan's madrassa teacher had said.

As the crowd waited, the globe began to spew more sparks. A thousand angels began to fly in circles around it, causing everyone to believe the globe was indeed the image of the one and only God Himself. Once, Suf-yan had asked his madrassa teacher if Allah would reveal Himself to humans on the Day of Judgment. The teacher had answered "No," which didn't make sense to Suf-yan. If the earth as we know it no longer existed, he had contemplated, then, what's the point of Allah's not manifesting Himself on that final day—even if to prove a point or humiliate those who had doubted His existence and power? Which would include Suf-yan himself.

A haphazard queue was soon formed at the bottom of the giant building. An Asian woman was the first in line, and as she waited for instructions from above, a shiny golden platform was lowered from the top of the building. The platform was not connected to the building itself and didn't seem to be suspended from any object. The woman walked forth boldly and stood on the platform. A siren went off somewhere from the sky, after which the platform shot up into the air like a rocket. It stopped about two-thirds of the way up the building and remained suspended in the air. The woman was then visible to the billions of humans, who with reverent, fearful eyes, waited for their turns.

The Asian woman stood erect, her naked body drenched with the rays of light from the sparks emitted from the globe.

"Wonders of God," muttered Suf-yan, as he marveled at the whole spectacle. In a ritual that would be repeated with every single human being present, the archangel circled the woman's head three times, then held his Palm Pilot in front of her, so she could see the contents. The archangel then announced to the woman, and by extension to everyone present, that she was welcome to challenge any entry on the Palm Pilot with which she didn't agree.

The woman took a quick glance and nodded her head in agreement to what was entered in the archangel's database. With his right hand the archangel raised his inkless pen and made a check sign in the air, indicating that this woman had been cleared to go to *Aljannah*. Two angels rushed to the platform and whisked her toward the main gate of Heaven, which was located in the distance behind and to the right of the Empire State Building. The gate of Hell was to the left of the building.

According to Suf-yan's madrassa teacher, Heaven was divided into seven different levels, with the lowest being where the least pious and honorable men and women were taken. Levels two through four were reserved for humans, too, but the fifth level, the highest any mortal could reach, would house people with the model moral and religious virtues, like prophets and their ilk. The sixth level would be where the angels and jinns were sent, while the seventh was the place Allah Himself dwelled, a place where not even the prophets were allowed. But on the other hand, Hell had only one huge chamber, though people would feel the fire's heat according to the extent of their sins.

As the Asian woman disappeared into the distance, Suf-yan couldn't help feeling pity for himself. He also wondered which level the woman was being sent to.

Like an automated shaft, the platform moved downward with the same speed it had taken the woman up. The next person was a tall, heavily bearded Arab man. And even before the angel had shown him his deeds, the man began to cry. "I know I have sinned," he cried and pleaded for God's forgiveness. But the angel would not hear any of it. He announced to the hearing of all, "Allah could forgive the sins you have committed against Him, but He cannot forgive those you have committed against your fellow man. And, my little human friend, I don't have to remind you of all the evil deeds you have committed against your fellow man."

The man cried, insisting he was ready to beg for forgiveness from the people he had wronged.

"You are going to have to go and pay for your sins in Hell until they have had the same chance to face the account of their life. If they are willing to forgive you, we'll retrieve you from the fire and ask the angels to transfer you to Heaven." The man was whisked to the gates of Hell before he could plead any further.

Next on the platform was a wiry black woman, whom Suf-yan identified as the Caribbean evangelist who always preached about Jesus's love and Hell's raging fire on the Q train. The woman was sent to Heaven for her religious deeds and also for her "clean, uncorrupted heart." She was followed by an adulterous man who was also greedy and miserly. The angels were so eager to send the man to Hell, they could hardly wait for the archangel's Hell sign-off, which was in the form of a cross.

In what seemed like only a few minutes, the cases of hundreds of thousands of people were adjudicated. People were either sent to Hell or to Heaven, depending on either their deeds on earth or God's mercy. Each of Suf-yan's grandparents, his mother and father, and two aunts were sent to Heaven. One uncle was sent to Hell, for cheating on his wife and also for abusing his children. And in a baffling case of God's discretional judgment, another uncle, Uncle Hassan, who was a drunk all his life, was sent to Heaven. "For seven full days Allah will reject the prayers of the man who has sipped even a drop of alcohol," Suf-yan's teacher had once told his class. And knowing how often Uncle Hassan got drunk, Suf-yan had thought there was no way his uncle was going to Heaven. Uncle Hassan himself knew that, and consequently, he didn't even attempt to plead for forgiveness in front of the archangel. He was as stoic and calm as a stone, and seemed to have resigned himself to his fate. So, when the angel announced that, "Your drinking alcohol didn't harm anyone, and since you did it to hide from your sorrows, Allah, in His infinite mercy, has decreed that you be sent to Heaven, though with one condition: that you shall never enjoy or have even a taste of the wine provided in Heaven." Uncle Hassan was so joyous of the verdict, he broke down in tears and cried all the way to the gates of Heaven.

When it finally became Suf-yan's turn, he boarded the platform thinking he was finished. He wished he could see Pas-cal one more time before he was sent to Hell, even if to know what her fate was. But he cared less about his first wife, whose good deeds and religious conviction, he was convinced, would earn her an easy ticket to Heaven.

Suf-yan gave a cursory glance at the bulleted points on the Palm Pilot and nodded to the archangel that he was ready. The archangel lifted his massive, feathery hand slowly, and instead of the sign of the cross Suf-yan had anticipated, the angel made the check sign with his inkless pen.

Suf-yan was in shock, and although exhilarated beyond description, found himself frozen. He felt like he'd won a lottery. But just as the angel was going to hand Suf-yan over to the two angels who escorted people to their final destinations, loud screams were heard from below. Suf-yan looked down and saw three people—with fists raised high up in the air—screaming at the top of their lungs, "His verdict was all a mistake."

It was the first time God's judgment was being protested by anyone since the judgment proceedings began, so there was great confusion on the ground. Even the archangel himself seemed shocked. He opened his owl-eyes widely, and was about to raise his hand when a thunderous laughter was heard from the globe, followed by a million sparks of light that rained on the crowd. The archangel then invoked three golden platforms, which he immediately dispatched to receive the three protesters.

When the men were raised up, Suf-yan was flabbergasted to see that all three were his childhood madrassa friends, Samad, Razak, and Kabir. The last time Suf-yan saw the trio was eighteen years ago, on a visit to Ghana. Even then, they denounced him as an infidel when they heard about his life in New York. And being hard-core extreme Islamists, they had refused to talk to Suf-yan for the remaining days of his visit, invoking the fundamentalist tenet that barred *mu-mins* (steadfast Muslims) from having anything to do with infidels and Muslims who have gone astray of their religious upbringing.

The three men were then asked by the archangel to tell the great gathering why they objected to Suf-yan's admission to Heaven.

"Why is this man going to Heaven? It must be a mistake," they chorused. "This man ate pork, lived and conducted business with nonbelievers, didn't even believe that a day like this would ever arrive, and on top of all that, he was a nonbeliever, too."

A hush fell over the crowd as the archangel quietly contemplated the trio's indictments. He looked directly at the globe, apparently waiting for divine instruction.

The archangel faced the trio and asked, "Has this man ever done anything to harm your persons?"

"No," the three replied.

"Has he ever made use of your wives?"

"No."

"Has he ever done anything treacherous to any of you, like backbiting or selling you to an enemy?"

"No," answered the three men.

The archangel turned and looked at Suf-yan. He lifted his hand in the air and repeated the same check sign he had made earlier. Then he turned and looked at the three dejected men, lifted his hand as slowly as he could above their heads, as if waiting for everyone present to see, then made the sign of the cross, sentencing them all to Hell. They bawled uncontrollably as they were marched toward Hell's large gates.

A few moments later Suf-yan was taken to the third level of

Heaven, to a round self-contained two-bedroom cottage situated in the middle of a lavish garden that smelled of roses, zinnias, and hundreds of lovely flowers he had never set eyes on before. On one side of the house was a natural lake for his private use, and on the other side, a garden filled with every kind of fruit and vegetable that ever existed. The sky was ocean-blue, the breeze sweet, and the sun golden. Everything about his final resting place in Heaven was just as perfect as his madrassa teacher had disclosed.

A dozen angels, to whom God had given access to the pulse of his heart and mind, were dispatched to satisfy Suf-yan's every need. He simply had to wish for anything at all, and there it was before his thought was even completed. "Such is the power and will of Allah," Suf-yan's madrassa teacher had once said, "who, as a reward for our good deeds, has created a Heaven where there is no aging or sickness, no heartaches or sadness, no hunger or thirst."

So, there in his heavenly estate, Suf-yan lived forever and ever.

MAN PASS MAN

1.

Zongo Street was full of idle men. They slept during the day and stayed up through the night, gossiping at Mallam Sile's tea shop or in front of Mansa BBC's—the street's most prominent gossip—kiosk. The idlers earned a living through swindling and gambling, and spent whatever they made on *akpeteshie*, a cheap but very strong brandy. When they failed to make any money through their strong-arm methods, the idlers often resorted to begging for alms or stealing food in the market-place. One of these guys was Suraju, who had a reputation as the greatest swindler and best drunkard on Zongo Street.

His father, a drunkard himself, had died after he had won a big drinking contest. Suraju was only fifteen at the time. Then his mother also died, barely eight months after her husband's death. The poor woman's demise was no doubt hastened by her anguish at the alcoholism of her husband's and son's. She was one of the kindest women to have ever lived on Zongo Street, and was referred to as *mai hasken zuciya*, or the bright-hearted one. But rather unfortunately, her parents had given her away in marriage when she was only fifteen—to Suraju's father, who was twenty-five then and managing a provision store near the Nkrumah market.

Suraju started drinking when he was quite young. It was rumored that his father secretly drank with him at night, after his mother had gone to sleep. By the time he was twelve, Suraju was already drinking akpeteshie as older men did. Now at twenty-six, he looked like someone in his late thirties. Suraju was tall and skinny, as skinny as a millet-grinding pestle, and had a slightly protruding belly, resembling a kwashiorkor patient. Still, he had the most beautiful pair of eyes on Zongo Street. They were white and large, their pupils as black as charcoal. His eyebrows were full, with long and silky eyelashes.

Suraju lived only for the moment. On the days he made money from swindling, he dressed elegantly and ate at expensive "chop bars" in the town proper. And on the days he wasn't lucky, and "caught crab instead of fish," he was found haggling at Mallam Sile's tea shop, pawning his clothes for a cup of tea and a loaf of bread from the half-blind tea seller.

After his parents' deaths, Suraju sold the house he had inherited from them and in less than six months, squandered half the money on akpeteshie. The rest he spent on the *ashawo* women at Efie-Nkwanta, an old brothel on Bompata Road. After splurging the money, Suraju somehow managed to squeeze a loan out of Asika, the tight-fisted moneylender on Zongo Street. With the loan, Suraju paid Afedzi Carpenter, another lazy drunkard, to build him a plywood shack on an abandoned strip of land located between Roman Hill and Zongo Street. He called his new abode "No Man's Land." And it had no furniture, except a kapok bed and two cardboard boxes, in which he kept his few belongings.

Once, Suraju was unable to come up with new frauds and was broke for more than two weeks. Finally, he concocted a fake drug, which he made out of finely ground corn, juices extracted from cassava, odum tree bark, spinach juice, and some saccharin. He went around Zongo Street and its adjacent neighborhoods peddling this nostrum. He convinced old people it would add another twenty years to their lives. Suraju was able to keep the whole scam a secret by telling his victims not to disclose to anyone—under any circumstance—that they were using the drug. He threatened them, and warned that their doing so would render the medicine ineffective and might even cause an early death.

He made some money selling that stuff until one of his victims, an old woman who lived on Zerikyi Road, denounced him. The woman, who suffered from rheumatism, had apparently gotten sicker after she had started using Suraju's "life-prolonging" pills. Many were those who chided the old woman for not only buying the so-called medicine but believing the bogus story behind it. "She should've known better," people said. Yet they all knew they were not beyond succumbing to Suraju's powers of persuasion. Many of the streetfolks believed he had a black-magic charm and that he could even sell people the very underwear they had on. During the time of his drug scam, Suraju was nicknamed "*Mallam mai Mágani*," or the Doctor of Medicine.

After the scam had lost its customers, Suraju was again left without a means of income. Finally he turned to stealing little items around the neighborhood, like the aluminum cooking pots left overnight in the courtyard of houses on the street. He sold them to Dan Tsoho, the blacksmith, who melted the pots and pans to make rain gutters. But despite all this, Suraju was still treated nicely by the streetfolks, some of whom even adored him. Their sympathy stemmed from something that had happened many years before Suraju had been born. His grandfather had murdered an *akpeteshie* seller and stolen her money; and the husband of his victim was said to have made an offering of a sheep to a fetish priest, who in turn cursed the grandfather and all his male descendants—the reason Suraju had ended up being the swindler and drunkard he was.

Suraju was especially adored by the street's old folks, even though they were, ironically enough, the main victims of his numerous scams. The old people never considered him a real thief, claiming that he stole simply to afford his "chop money." He was also a favorite among the kids—especially the delinquents, to whom he was a hero. Most of them admired Suraju's slickness— his ability to get away with almost any fraud. Now, the boys on Zongo Street were well known in all of Kumasi for their harsh, vicious treatment of the drunks they came across. They pelted them with rotten eggs, orange husks, or rocks. At times, too, they beat them with sticks and dragged them into the gutter, forcing filthy water down their throats. Though Suraju was drunk quite often, he was never treated in such a crude manner. Perhaps it was because of his fondness for these kids. He gathered them together after school and told them stories of his exploits, which he called *op'rayshan*. Many of the kids in return were equally fond of the swindler. They admired his deftness in making quick money, and because of that, followed him everywhere—especially when he caught fish.

Zongo Street was situated at the very end of the Muslim section of Kumasi. It bordered Roman Hill, where the Christian section—to the west of the city—began. The Roman "Hillians" were mainly Asantes and Christians, while the Zongolese comprised the Hausa, Mossi, Wangara, Zabarma, and Yoruba tribes, all northern Muslim tribes from Nigeria, Burkina Faso, and Mali. And despite the differences in religion and ethnicity, the two communities lived in perfect harmony. In fact about half of the students at St. Peter's, the Catholic primary and middle schools that were located in Roman Hill, were from Zongo Street. The vast playgrounds and soccer fields of the fifteen-acre diocese compound was opened to Christian and Muslim kids alike, and they played there together after school. And Suraju, being the darling of the delinquent kids on the street, was always found hanging around the church compound, with them in tow.

One hot sunny afternoon in November, Suraju was sitting in front of the Roman Catholic church, spinning some of his many exploits into tales for the kids, when Anoma, a well-known witch from Roman Hill, walked past. Anoma the witch was very old and scrawny, with a multitude of wrinkles on her face. She was wearing her usual white-calico robe, and holding her old walking stick. As soon as Anoma was out of sight, Suraju stopped telling his tale. He quickly began buckling on his sandals, ready to depart. The boys grabbed his sleeve and asked why he was leaving, but Suraju only continued buckling his sandals, not paying any attention to them. He hummed an unknown tune noiselessly and shook his head in swift motions. The boys insisted that he tell them why he suddenly wanted to leave. One of them, whose mother sold *akpeteshie*, promised to steal a bottle of the drink for Suraju if he stayed and continued with his story.

"Give it up, boys," said Suraju, tugging his sleeve away. "No one is going to hear about this one. No-no-no-no-no-no, no. No one. This is my secret new plan," he mumbled silently to himself. "This is my last chance to become rich," he continued. "Man, it appears like God is now ready to put butter on both sides of my bread!" A wide grin appeared on Suraju's face, followed by a triumphant laugh. He jumped to his feet in celebration and ran off down the steps of the church and down onto the road that led to the market square, leaving the dumbfounded children on the stairs, watching him disappear.

Suraju was seen at a market stall the following day, buying white calico from a trader. Later, the market woman claimed Suraju had bought twelve yards from her, and that he had refused to disclose what he was using it for, which caused a chain of rumors to erupt about what "the king of swindlers" was actually up to this time. During the week that followed, Suraju was not seen much on the street, and when he was spotted, he seemed very busy, only waving without stopping.

Now, that was quite abnormal for Suraju, who would usually start up a conversation even if there were nothing to converse about. Thrice during the same week, he was seen at Inuwa the Tailor's shop. And on all three occasions, he and Inuwa had disappeared into the private inner chamber of the shop. "Inuwa and I, we have a *biz-ness* to do. You folks just have to wait and you may be lucky to see what it is," Suraju repeated to those who had seen him and insisted that he disclose what he was doing with the tailor. Before this, Suraju had been known for revealing the secrets of his frauds, especially when he was drunk. Therefore the streetfolks were confident that sooner or later he would start "running his mouth" about his already famous "secret new plan."

A few days after he was last spotted at Inuwa the Tailor's, Suraju was seen with the usual throng of kids at his heels, heading toward the market. But what was seen of the swindler was not the Suraju the streetfolks had always known, even when he had plenty of money. He was dressed in an expensive Arabian silk suit and wearing a pair of handmade leather sandals to match. His neck was adorned with gold and silver necklaces, and he sported gold-rimmed sunglasses. By the end of the week that followed, it became quite obvious that Suraju was making lots of money from some mysterious source. His pockets were stuffed with rolls and rolls of cedi notes. He stopped food vendors at the central market, paid for the entire stock they carried, and distributed it among the dusty mendicants by the roadside. With his fellow conmen, Suraju squandered lots of money and bought them *akpeteshie* at Apala Goma, a local drinking shack.

The teenage girls on Zongo Street benefited the most from Suraju's "money rain." He spent generously on them, taking the young women to Prempeh Hall, where they watched the nightly dance and drama performances. He lavished expensive gifts on them: gold necklaces, lavender perfumes, and the latest blouses in fashion. In the evenings he took the girls to Doula's, a popular meat kiosk on Zerikyi Road, where he treated them to *balango*, a special beef kebab made with varieties of hot spices and groundnut paste. This was the kind of food only the rich in Kumasi could afford. It was even rumored—and this came directly from Mansa BBC's kiosk—that Suraju had bought a set of gold trinkets for Safiya, a girl he liked. The kids who had done Suraju favors when he was broke also got their share. He bought meat pies and Fanta drinks for them in the late afternoons, after their return from school.

The street's elderly were not left out in Suraju's spending spree, either. He bought a headscarf and a pair of sandals each for the old women he was acquainted with in the neighborhood, probably to atone for past swindles foisted upon them. This particular generosity caused the biggest stir on the street, creating numerous speculations about his source of income, which still remained a mystery. Not even Jawara, Suraju's longtime comrade, knew where the money was coming from. Mansa BBC claimed Suraju was a member of a gang that looted banks and shops at night in the town proper. The streetfolks knew BBC's reputation for creating juicy stories out of thin air, and so took her version with a grain of salt.

Day in and day out, Suraju's spending spree continued. He would throw handfuls of cedi coins in the air, urging kids and beggars to jump and grab them. "Enjoy it while it lasts, my friends, enjoy it!" he would say as he tossed the money. "After all, what is money made for but to spend." Before long, Suraju's nickname was changed from "the king of swindlers" to "Alhaji Richman." Kids on the street, using the new nickname, cheered him as he walked past. He would wave a white handkerchief, and then throw more cedi coins in the air.

As time went by, the street became alarmed by the swindler's continuous profligacy. People wondered where he could have gotten the money he threw around left and right, like a farmer throws millet to his chicks. Mallam Sile, once, in his polite, timid manner, asked Suraju how he came into that much money. Suraju became quite annoyed at the tea seller's question and said harsh words to poor Mallam Sile, calling him "*kwata tu wan,*" or a "quarter to one," a phrase that alluded to Sile's blind eye. "All you people on this street are jealous of my success, because of your poverty!" he went on to say.

After the tea shop incident, people became hesitant to ask Suraju about his dealings, though dozens of new stories were being fabricated each day about him. By now, some on the street had begun to believe BBC's earlier speculation—the one that claimed Suraju was a night burglar. Others, however, believed he had acquired the money either through gambling or a much bigger scam. Quite a number of the superstitious types believed Suraju had a "black-magic" snake hidden under his bed, and it vomited twenty thousand cedis for him every night.

"That Suraju boy is by all means milking a wild bull for all this money, but he will rue the day he was born when he milks it dry, for the bull will certainly attack and eat him alive," muttered an old woman who happened to be one of those who didn't get a scarf or a pair of sandals from Suraju.

"Ninety-nine days for the thief, the hundredth for the owner," said Wanzami, the caretaker of the street's central mosque. "His days are numbered," Wanzami concluded.

Despite the anxiety some people harbored for Suraju, others were quite happy for him. The housewives were especially glad that the minor thefts that used to occur in the neighborhood had stopped since Suraju began to "earn a living for himself." They rejoiced over the fact that their aluminum cooking utensils remained right where they had left them the previous night. But as days passed, people's anxiety about Suraju turned into fear. Everyone hoped that the truth would be known sooner rather than later. And with no other alternative, the streetfolks waited for the day "the smoke would force the rat from its hole."

Suraju's day of reckoning came one night during the early days of harmattan. It was chilly and dry as usual during this time of the year, and not a single soul was seen outdoors, except a small group made up of the street's conmen and juvenile delinquents. They sat around a log fire in front of the Zongo chief's assembly shed, eating roasted groundnuts while they spun tales.

Suddenly the group heard loud screams from a distance. They stopped and listened attentively, trying to determine the direction from which it was coming. It did not take long for them to recognize the screamer's high-pitched voice to be Suraju's. He screamed, "Man Pass Man! Help! Man Pass Man!"

Moments later Suraju came running; he gasped for breath, like a wounded deer. He fell to the ground some few meters away from the group and continued screaming, "Man Pass Man! Help! Man Pass Man! Save me, O!" The men looked around, to make sure nobody was following him. And to their relief, it appeared no one was in sight.

Suddenly Suraju became silent, growing stiff. His alarmed comrades ran in circles around him, not knowing what to do.

"He is dying," said one of them.

"No, he is not. Maybe he has passed out," said Jawara.

"What do you mean by that? I say, look. He is dying, can't you see his face?" screamed another.

"*Oya*, now, Charlie Men. We can't waste time. Go fetch some water," shouted Jawara.

The party ran off on hearing the command, leaving only Jawara and another young man to look after Suraju. They rushed to the nearest compound and grabbed as many buckets as they could find, waking up half the tenants with their noises. Then they dashed to a nearby public pipe and filled the buckets with water. Ignoring the coolness of the night, they dumped the cold water all over Suraju, hoping that would make him regain consciousness. Suraju screamed and made a slight movement with his knees, as though he was trying to sit up. He fell back to the wet ground, where he remained sprawled—as if dead.

2.

News—bad news especially—traveled very fast on Zongo Street. Within a few moments of this occurrence, half the sleeping street had been informed, and very soon folks began to pour out of their tenement houses and shanties to the scene. In less than ten minutes there was a crowd of about twenty, and many kept coming afterward. Newcomers stretched their necks and tried to catch a glimpse of Suraju, who lay flat on his belly, with arms outstretched in opposite directions.

"Poor boy," said the cobbler's wife. "Some cruel *al-janni* is definitely responsible for this," she added.

"*They* are torturing him. God protect this child," lamented another elderly woman.

"Look, people. I think it is hunger that is causing all this," said the cobbler, a huge chewing stick tucked at one corner of his mouth. "Perhaps he should be given some food!" the cobbler suggested. A woman ran swiftly to her house and returned a few moments later with a bowl of *hura da nono*, millet porridge prepared with fresh goat milk. Jawara and another young man turned the swindler on his back and helped him to sit up. After much prodding Suraju opened his eyes; the bowl was handed to him. He downed the porridge in three quick gulps, and instantly a gleam of consciousness appeared on his face.

"May I have some more?" he asked in a weak voice.

"You see, I told you it was hunger!" said the cobbler, beaming.

The woman once again scurried back to her house, and moments later, returned with a bigger bowl of the porridge. Suraju finished the fresh bowl as soon as it was handed to him. He let out a weak belch and remained seated on the wet ground. He stared suspiciously at the people in the crowd, who in turn looked back at him—as if he were a rare beast of some sort. Then suddenly, as if frightened by something he alone had seen, Suraju covered his face with both hands and began screaming, "Man Pass Man! Man Pass Man! I done die, O! Man Pass Man!"

"Okay, shut up your big mouth now, you rascal," shouted Wanzami. "The time has come for you to stop your nonsense and tell us what is happening!"

Wanzami was skinny and bald-headed, and in his mid-seventies. Yet he was fierce and very energetic. He had a countenance that resembled an eagle's: pensive and voracious, and was known all across the street and beyond for his habit of judging and talking about other people's shortcomings—as a result of which he had been nicknamed "Razor-mouth." Wanzami was widowed and had two grown daughters, both of whom had produced "bastard children." And on more than three occasions, he had been suspected of using money from the mosque's collection box for his own private use. But fearing his razor mouth, no one dared question Wanzami about those allegations or even speak about his promiscuous daughters in public.

Suraju did not respond to Wanzami's taunts. He stared quizzically at the caretaker as if it were the first time he was seeing him.

"Be soft on him, Wanzami," the cobbler's wife bravely spoke up. "This child has suffered enough, as it is! Can't you see his condition? Be gentle with him, for Allah's sake. You know very well that what is happening to him is not from his own doing. It is the spirits that have taken over his senses!"

"Look here, woman. Don't tell me what you don't know, okay? Whose doing is it then if it is not his? And who told you I care about what happens to this rogue?" Wanzami roared, flipping his wiry arms in the air.

The crowd became silent, casting all its attention on the swindler. After a while, Suraju began to clear his throat, and for the first time that night spoke intelligibly to the crowd.

"By God, I will tell you everything that has happened in the past few weeks. And after hearing the story of what took place tonight, of what I saw, you will agree with me that, yes, Man Pass Man." Breathing heavily, Suraju went on, and his voice rose. "You will also agree with me that, indeed, some ghosts strong pass other ghosts. I am speaking about real ghosts here, folks. They are everywhere! I swear to my God that I saw one tonight, *kirikiri* with my two eyes. I see one coming right now. Help! Save me, O! He is coming to get me, O! I done die, O!" He screamed hysterically, leaving the crowd even more confused.

"What are you talking about? What is it about ghosts?"

Jawara asked. He grabbed Suraju by the arms and shook him violently.

"Look, either you tell us what is happening to you or we leave. Right now! Can't you tell it is too cold for us to be standing out here, you rogue?" shouted Wanzami in his nasal, condescending voice.

"Have patience, man," said Suraju, finally opening his eyes.

"Who are you calling 'man,' eh? Who is your 'man'? Do you think I am your equal? You have no respect in those eyes of yours, calling me 'man'!" shouted Razor-mouth.

"Have patience," Suraju interjected in a soft yet firm voice. "I was the one who made the promise to tell you what has been cooking in my pot, and I can decide not to tell it. But I will not fail your ears tonight. Trust me. You only have to be a little patient with me, and you will all know about my secret plan. Now, for us to enjoy this 'news,' I'll say we add more logs to the fire, and get more groundnuts and water, to keep our engine running."

Hardly had Suraju finished this sentence when people dashed to their houses, some to get their blankets, others to fetch groundnuts and drinking water. On their return, they tried to move as close as they possibly could to the center, where Suraju sat, to grab every bit of the story about to be told. Meanwhile a couple of Suraju's comrades carted dry logs, which they had righteously stolen from Baba Salisu—the wood seller's—shed. Within a few minutes the air was alit by the rising flame of the fire.

. . .

"It all began about three weeks ago," Suraju started slowly. He sat on a wooden stool offered to him by someone in the crowd. His entire body, from feet to chin, was wrapped in an old blanket provided by the cobbler's wife.

"One afternoon I was telling stories to my little friends in front of Roman Chu'ch when that witch-woman, Anoma, came and walked past where we sat. She was wearing that dirty white gown she wears like a *sukoo* uniform. But as soon as Anoma walked past us now, some good idea come jump into my head. Man, before you can say *go-come*, ideas began to pour in and out of my head like a gourd spilling over with *akpeteshie* again and again. But folks, the truth is that even before I saw Anoma I had been thinking of new ways to make my own 'chop money,' so that I would stop duping or stealing from you. So, when that idea came and jumped into my head now, I knew I could use it to start a quick-money op'rayshan. And it was all the more crazy because it was Anoma's dirty white gown that started everything. Just think that!"

"Was that why you bought the white calico from the market?" asked Aliko the barber.

"I beg you, *lawya-man*, I don't have time for your questions, O," interjected Suraju. "I don't have time, you heard me so? You ask too many questions, we all go sleep here."

Many in the crowd looked contemptuously at Aliko the barber, a puny, middle-aged man who had a penchant for arguing. Aliko could argue with you about anything under the sun and have the upper hand, even if he knew nothing about the issue at stake.

"So, I rushed home after I saw Anoma," Suraju continued. "I

lay on my bed the whole afternoon. I thought and thought and thought, trying to find a good plan that will work with my new idea." Almost everyone present knew Suraju didn't have a bed in his room, but they allowed him to proceed, as he couldn't be challenged at that moment. "After two days had passed, I came up with a very, very good plan. On that same day I went to the market and bought me twelve yards of *alkwado*. I gave the cloth to Inuwa to sew me a robe. And he made me a good one; it covered all my body, from head to toe, face and all, except the three little holes he made for my eyes and mouth. Man, if you see me in that robe, you wouldn't be able to tell me from a true ghost."

There was a big hush as Suraju spoke. Other than his voice, no sound was heard except a deep cough, which everyone knew came from Hamda One, the street's latrine man.

"I wasted no time after Inuwa had finished sewing my robe. I began the op'rayshan that same day. When night came—I remember well, well that it was a Friday night—I gathered my tools, a *baafu* [penknife], a to'ch light, and a skoo dry-va. I carried them all in one small *raw-bah* bag, together with the ghost uniform. I left home just before ten o'clock, and I first went to Standa'd Bank to take the *trotro* to Kejetia *rah-nah-bout*. When I reached the town proper now, I walked around the lorry park and looked at the big shop windows until I hear the po 'soffice clock tower strike at midnight. That was the hour I started the op'rayshan.

"First I would find me one dark road, where I could stop a taksi without the dryba seeing my face. I am sure you think me mad, or something, and ask why I took this precaution, but you shall soon understand why I did that. Most of them taksi men in this our city, you'self know already, don't like driving the cemetery route when darkness enters. But the funny thing was, the cemetery was the exact place I wanted them to take me to. So, what did I do? I would promise to pay them five hundred cedis on top of the charge, which made their mouths drool!

"First thing I did when I climbed into the backseat was to throw salute to the dryba. I would say in my Ingilish broka, 'Charlie Man, how t'ings dey go now?' But every one of them stupid drybas, minus the devil I stopped tonight, gave me the same reply: 'T'ings no dey bad, my broda. How for do? So long as man dey live, t'ings go com' better some day.' What annoyed me was that they refused to shut up their mouths after that—you know them taksi drybas already! They would go on and on about their money palavers and sufferings, as if I was God's sacateray or his small brother or something. They blabbed about their nagging wives and their children's school fees, which they said was too dear to pay. Some of them complained—with real anger—about how things have become so expensive that common people like them cannot even buy a bottle of beer to quench their sorrows. Plenty of them did nothing but bitch about Cha'rman Rawlings, the Pres'dent. But I think it is all jealousy, no one wants to see anybody do better in life. They said the Pres'dent chops fatty meat and grows big belly and fat cheeks, while all they can afford is poor man's food, *kenkey* with hot pepper. But I knew all the while that the drybas told me their sufferings so I would feel pity and dash them extra money. They didn't know that I know all their tricks.

"Anyway, before we reach the cemetery, I would tell the dryba that my papa was just buried yesterday and that I was going to pray a special prayer for him. Some of them believed my stupid lie so much they even prayed for my papa to see the gates of Heaven. And the moment we reached the cemetery gate, I would jump out of the taksi, carrying my raw-bah bag with me. I would then walk all the way to the Muslim burial site, where I would quickly put the robe on top of my clothes. After that, I put the raw-bah bag and all the things in it in the big secret pocket inside the robe. Then slowly and quietly I would begin to walk back to the taksi. I must be honest and tell you that at this point I was as scared as a dog that was face-to-face with a lion. My heart would be beating, *dum pa, dum pa, dum pa pa, dum pa,* like, like *ganga* drum," Suraju stammered.

He took a short pause and unwrapped himself from the blanket, complaining it was too warm. People in the back raised and shifted their heads constantly, like lizards, so they could see his face properly. Those in the front row of the circle stared fixedly at the swindler, with mouths and nostrils widely open.

"By the time I walked back to the taksi, some of them stupid drybas would be dozing their heads off and snoring like hyenas. The cowards among them never slept, though—they were widely awake behind the *sitee-ya,* praying for me to show up. When I neared the gate, I knelt down on my knees and crawled to the back of the taksi, to make sure the dryba didn't see me in my robe. I remained quiet for a while, and would then pick up a few pieces of rocks and start throwing them at the taksi's glass. The dryba would jump and look around, very scared. I would throw some more rocks and then rise slowly from the ground, screaming 'moo-neey, moo-neey, moo-neey, moo-neey,' opening my mouth widely and stretching my arms forward as if I were going to strangle the dryba through the front glass. Thinking I was a ghost, the dryba would open the door and run for his life, shouting, 'Ghost! Ghost! Ghost!' I would stamp my feet heavily on the ground—to scare him even more and make him run faster. I would chase him off a little and return to the taski to finish the op'rayshan.

"Once I reenter the taksi, I removed my to'ch light from the raw-bah bag," Suraju's voice rose excitedly. "And flashed the light onto the dryba's side, looking for the cash box. As soon as I found it I emptied all the money into my raw-bah bag. On two or three nights, I couldn't open the damn cash box, and that was why I began to carry a skoo dry-va and my *baafu* with me. I never used my knife to stab or kill anyone, O! Like BBC said. I heard all about it, you know, she running around with her fat and useless buttocks, telling people that I was a bank robber!" The crowd roared with laughter.

"After I have cleared the cash box, I would leave the scene quick-quick," Suraju continued amidst the crowd's excited noises. "I ran and took a shortcut home through Kawo Kudi Jun'tion, where I stopped to take off the robe. It was in this way that I carried out the op'rayshan each night, except that I took the taksis at different areas and suburbs in town proper, that way nobody could follow my shadow. So, my good people, that was how I made my 'chop money' for the past two or three weeks. And everything had gone according to plan, until the big crab I caught tonight."

Suraju paused and asked for water and groundnut. Two bowls, one containing groundnuts and the other water, were hastily passed to him. People exchanged glances while he drank the water. The crowd seemed surprised, not believing their ears that Suraju had actually gotten away with robbing the city's taxi drivers for more than two weeks. A middle-aged man in the crowd admitted to having heard about a ghost that had been haunting taxi drivers in the city, but had never thought it was Suraju. The listeners, though a bit spooked, were nonetheless even more curious and eager to hear about the "crab" that caught Suraju on this fateful night.

"The moment I sat in the taksi I picked tonight I smelled trouble!" Suraju continued, his mouth full of groundnuts. "But, as the elders say, 'One who is destined to receive a sound beating never listens to words of caution!' This taksi, now, didn't look like those half-dead taksis you see around this our city. Man, it looked like it just came out of the factir, with many different colors of light inside and outside, like a moving disco. The chair and everything inside was white; it even had a ster'o. Strange for this our town, eh? I was surprised and scared at the same time, but my mind was already thinking about the loot under the dryba's seat. And so I went ahead.

"I threw my everyday salute to the dryba as I sat in the back. I would say, 'How t'ings dey go for you now, ol' boy?'

"I didn't hear any answer.

"Maybe he is deaf or dumb or the two together," I said in my head.

"I shouted another salute to him; very, very loud, this one. But the *mumu* refused to say even one word back to me. He acted as if I weren't in his car a-tall a-tall. I come regret taking the taksi now, because my nose began to smell trouble right there.

"For a while now, the taksi dryba and I didn't say even *hun* to each other. I just sat in the backseat and looked through the window, counting the stores and houses on the streets of Ash Town. Though I was very scared, greediness still pushed me to go on with the op'rayshan. I began to plan how to do it, but then I come realize that before I start anything a-tall, I must tell the dryba where I wanted him to take me. But just as I was about to open my mouth, he said to me: 'Don't worry, bo-boy. I know where you are going.' When I heard that, Charlie Man, I began to sweat like a he-goat trying to climb his wife, Madame She-goat. I said to myself: Kai, man must be inside some big *wahala* today, O! If shithole doesn't burst open tonight, it go crack, at least!

"A little moment came and passed, and still the *mumu* would not talk—he wouldn't even look at me in his 'look-back' mirror. I was thinking what to say to him, though I knew he would not reply. Then all of a sudden he asked, 'Where do you want to be taken to tonight? The cemetery?' Man, I almost shit in my 'sporter' when he asked that question. Fear came and grabbed me so tight I couldn't even answer him. He turned around and asked me the same question again. And that was when I saw his face. You have to see it to believe it! His neck was like yam tuber, large and long. His upper and lower teeth were jagged, like the end of sharpened pencils. They also looked very white and clean. His nose looked like banana run over by a bicycle tire. His ears, folks, were bigger than a rabbit's, and his eyeballs looked like they were going to jump out of their shells. Believe me, that devil was the ugliest creature I have ever seen in my life! To tell you the truth, he was even uglier than Bona." A roar of laughter erupted from the crowd, followed by a scuffle between Bona's concubine—a fat, pot-bellied middle-aged man—and a teenager who had laughed hysterically at Suraju's joke.

"Listen here, you two. Either you quit this fight or I stop, *nownow*! I am tired already," shouted Suraju. The scuffle ceased as suddenly as it had started, and all attention was once again directed at the Swindler.

"Then the next thing I heard was a funeral song coming from the speakers behind me. The song started very low, *smallsmall*, but it got louder and louder until my head began to shake, *jigi-jigi-jigi*. I screamed at him, 'Bring down your speakers! Bring down your speakers a little!' But it was as if I was talking to a pillar. No answer. Then all at once he shouted over the loud funeral song, 'Dead people are my people. They are my friends. I hate living people.' Charlie Man, that was when I come realize that I was inside a hot bowl of soup. My ears were red hot—they were hotter than fire itself. I began to think of how to escape! I wanted to fly out through the window, but your man didn't have the guts to do it. And so, I remained in the seat.

"We were nearing Magazin' Jun'tion by now. Small time passed, and I still couldn't come up with any escape plan. I decided to scream when we reach the Jun'tion, so that the people waiting for the trotro would hear me and come to my rescue. And it was then I came to believe that the dryba was a mind reader. The devil already knew about my plan to scream, and so just as I was about to open my mouth, he increased his speakers and began to drive faster. I sat in the right corner of the backseat, and placed my two palms between my knees, like a coup plotter being taken to the firin' squa'.

"At Magazin' Jun'tion I saw some people walking around, while others were standing in a trotro line. I tried to roll the windows down and shout for help. But the stubborn glass 'said' it wouldn't go anywhere. Kai, I waved my arms to them people outside. Nobody noticed me. I gave up and stopped waving. I shouted at the dryba, 'Stop, stop! Let me get off here! Right here, I say! I am no longer going to the cemetery, O! Hey, I don't even know where the grave of my dead papa is located, O! I say, I say, let me get off *now now*, O! My dead papa is still alive, O!' But the devil acted like I wasn't even in the car. He drove even faster and faster, and moved his head sideways—from left to right and from right to left, singing along with the funeral music.

"'Then, folks, what would I see next but smoke coming out of his ears and nostrils! Let Aradu's ax strike me dead if I am lying about this! It was thick smoke like that of burning forest. I screamed and pounded my fist on the window until my knuckles began to hurt. I closed my eyes and covered my nose with my open palms, but the smoke still found ways to enter my nose. It made me cough like someone with TB. Then all of a sudden, the devil began to scream, '*moo-neey, moo-neey, mooooo-neeeeey, neeeeey-mooooo, mooooo, mooooo-neeeeey.*' He changed his voice into a woman's and then back to a man's. '*Moo-neey, moo-neey,*' he kept on. At this point I knew that mine was finished and done with in this life, and that I was dead meat already. I began to chant, calling upon all my dead ancestors to come and save their son. I prayed for help from Allah Himself. I promised Him that if He rescued me, I would never dupe or swindle anyone ever again. I even vowed to quite drinking if He saved my life. I realized *quick-quick* that my ancestors and Allah Himself were not minding me a-tall, a-tall, because the car kept flying like a'roplane."

Suraju paused briefly and continued after clearing his throat and taking a sip of water. "So, I sat and waited for death-angel Azará-il to come and take me! I prayed and asked for forgiveness from everyone on this our street, especially the people I have duped and stolen from before. I asked Allah to forgive me for all the *akpeteshie* I drank in my whole life, and was ready to face my maker. Then suddenly I heard the sound of a big crash. At first I thought we had crashed into a tree or something really huge. My head hit the ceiling and front seat many times before the taksi came to a stop. All was quiet for a short time. No funeral song, no nothing. My body shook like fish out of water. I closed my eyes very tight and remained in the backseat for God knows how long. Then I began to hear the cries of an owl coming from a distance. That spooked me, you know, and so I opened my eyes. I looked all around me—front, back, left, and right. No dryba. And outside, it was very dark. So I tried to open the car door, but the useless thing said it, too, owned its own self—it refused to move. I heard footsteps shortly after that. I looked through the back glass, and what did I see but the taksi dryba. I almost fainted when he walked to my side and opened the door and asked me to step out. Tiredness didn't let me move even a limb; it was as if my body was nailed to the seat. He spoke in a low voice and told me that he wouldn't hurt me. He said he was my friend, and that I should step out of the taksi. I didn't trust him a bit. But since I had no power, I obeyed him. I was planning to take to my heels the moment my feet touched the ground. Instead, I fell down. Then everything vanished from my head.

"I was on the ground for God knows how long, and I can't tell you if I was just asleep or if I passed and the devil dryba took me to the land of the dead. But all of a sudden I began to see all the dead people who used to live here on Zongo Street. They came and passed in front of me, one by one. They made silly faces at me, their tongues sticking out and eyes wide open as if they'd seen a ghost. Papa Goldsmith was among the people I saw in the land of the dead. I also saw Yensuro, the palm wine taper—he was drunk as hell. I saw Papa Carpenter, my friend Afedzi's father. I saw Mallam Bawa the carrion-eater, and I even saw my dead papa—he was eating roasted sheep carrion and drinking *akpeteshie* with Mallam Bawa. That place I saw them dead people looked dirty and smelled very badly. But they all looked merry, like they were having a jolly time. That place I saw them, O! Hah, I think that place was Hell, O! You know why I said so? Because my dead mama was not there with them!

"Hunn," some in the crowd murmured profoundly, shaking their heads.

"After a long, long time, my eyes began to open bit by bit. I realized that I had left the land of the dead. When my eyes and the darkness became one, I come see that I was in the middle of the Tafo Cemetery, not far from the big *goji* tree in the Muslim section. I looked around; not a single soul was near. The dryba himself was not around. I looked up and thanked my God, and with my reserve *power*, I got up and rushed to the taksi. I searched for the raw-bah bag and found it. I removed the to'ch light and flashed it. All I saw were graves and tombstones.

"By God, he is a true ghost, then. Man Pass Man, indeed! I said in my head. There and then I threw the bag in the air, ready to fly. But a huge arm grabbed my waistband, my feet not touching the ground—the way police 'jack' pickpockets. It was the dryba. Again! I was too scared to even scream. He smiled through his jagged teeth and asked me to sit down on the grass. I obeyed him, my body shaking so. To God in Heaven, the sweat falling from my face was like rain shower—and let me not see tomorrow if I am lying!" The crowd was stiffly silent.

"The ghost then began to tell me all sorts of stories about himself when he was alive. But I cannot tell you most of things he said to me. He warned me *wellwell* not to give out certain important secrets he shared with me—even if someone gave me money and free akpeteshie for life."

No remark came from the listeners, and so Suraju continued.

"The ghost talked and talked and talked, his mouth going and coming like locomotive engine. Before he left, now, he asked if I would like him to give me the secret medicine that would make people come back to life after they die. I was afraid he might kill me and turn me into a ghost when I said yes, and so I asked him to give me time to think about the matter. He promised that if I return tomorrow, he will tell me a *bigbig* secret, and swore that if I knew this one secret, I could use it to become the richest man in this our city.

"Come now, ol' boy, tell us! What's the secret?" Jawara asked.

"He didn't tell me that one yet; I just told you. You see, ghosts are no fools either—he wants to make sure I go see him tomorrow night at the cemetery. And you know I am not stepping my feet there again, till the day I die. Still, he told me three smaller secrets I could use to get my 'chop money' for as long as I live. He talked on and on about his ghostfolks. He said it is jollier to live in the land of the dead than to live here on earth! According to him, *they* eat ten times each day and drink *akpeteshie* like we drink water down here. He said *they* don't even have to buy *akpeteshie* and Fanta and Coke in the land of the dead—they get them from special public taps. Just think that, Charlie Man! Free booze day and night, night and day. Ha-ha-ha!

"Folks, and just as he was preparing to leave, the ghost told me the most scariest story of them all. He said that half the people in this our city are ghosts, like himself. He swore by *his* dead mama's grave that *manymany* stalls and shops in the central market belong to ghost people. You know what that means, eh? We buy our foodstuffs from ghosts every day, and that also means we have been eating ghost food day by day. He even said there are *plentyplenty* ghosts on this our Zongo Street here, and he even named some names to me!" The listeners looked at each other askance, with distrustful glances, as if the person next to them was a ghost.

"Then the dryba suddenly stood up and said to me, 'I have the power to make you rich and powerful. But it is all up to you to seek it! Come see me tomorrow if you want to be immortal and rich. It is all up to you!' Before I could blink, the ghost dryba had vanished *kwatakwata*, just like that!

"I sat on the ground like a fat lazy cow. I was not sure if he was still playing cat and mouse with me, so I waited for some time to make sure he was not coming back. I continued to hear his voice for a long time; he was howling, 'You will become wealthy and powerful only when you know the secret! It is all up to you. Come back tomorrow!'

"I waited until all I heard was the *ze-ze-ze* sound of mosquitoes and some cricket noise. I looked all around me. No nothing! I borrowed the gazelle's legs. Charlie Man, I ran without thinking where I was headed. I was like a blind elephant running through the jungle—I hit and stepped over anything in my way. And before I knew it, I found myself here on Zongo Street. Only the Heavens could tell how that happened. Allah Himself must have brought me here on the wings of the angels, *Wallahi!*"

Suraju sighed heavily as he finished the story.

Whispers were heard here and there as people discussed the story. "So, when are you going to go meet the ghost for the big secret?" someone shouted from the noisy crowd. Suraju did not respond to the person. He merely shook his head and began to look nervously around him. He suddenly grabbed the blanket, and covering his face, began to scream, "There he goes again, O! People, the ghost dryba is here, O! He has come to get me, O! Help, help! Man Pass Man, Ghost Pass Ghost, O!" Within a blink of an eye, the crowd had dispersed. People ran helter-skelter in every direction, tripping and falling over each other. Many hollered as they fled, "*Ghost! Ghost! Ghost!*" as if they had actually seen one. Very soon not a single soul was found near the scene, except Suraju, who was curled up on the ground, with his head buried in his chest and the blanket draped over the top half of his body. He screamed repeatedly, "Man Pass Man! Man Pass Man! Man Pass Man!"